THE ORGANIZATION

ALLAN LEVERONE

THE ORGANIZATION

Copyright ©2014 by Allan Leverone

This is a work of fiction. Names, characters, places, and incidents either
are the product of the author's imagination or are used fictitiously.
Any resemblance to actual events, locales, or persons, living or dead, is
unintended and entirely coincidental.

Cover artwork and design by Elderlemon Design
Print edition formatting by JD Smith Design

1

Jack Sheridan had been parked at the curb near the Copley T station in Boston less than fifteen minutes when the car he was waiting for drove past. He felt a flash of annoyance that he had cut the timing so close; he would have preferred to be at least half an hour early.

Alone in the rental car, he shrugged. No matter. The important thing was that he hadn't missed his target.

Jack squinted and examined the right side of the weather-beaten blue Pontiac Le Mans as it cruised down Boylston Street. A long gouge, beginning on the passenger-side front door and continuing almost all the way to the taillight assembly, identified the car without question as the one he was waiting for.

The vehicle had been keyed at some point in the past, likely by an unsatisfied customer, a scratch that had bitten through every layer of paint, all the way down to bare metal. The damage had never been repaired, and now rust was eating its way steadily out of the furrow in all directions.

The Pontiac took an immediate right onto Dartmouth, just as Jack had expected it to, accelerating past the Boston Public Library. He waited a moment, allowing a couple of cars to fill in behind his quarry, and then he flipped on his turn signal and eased away from the curb. Traffic at this time of night was steady but not heavy, and it was an easy task to stay far enough behind the Le Mans that he wouldn't give away his presence to the unsuspecting driver.

The target drove with a practiced ease, taking exactly the rights and lefts Jack expected, and it became obvious the man was heading home.

Comfortable now that his expectations had been confirmed, Jack eased back another couple of car lengths and turned on the radio so that it was playing softly in the background. Through the speakers Brian Johnson screamed about getting shaken all night long. Against all odds, and probably common sense as well, the driving beat of hard rock always soothed Jack's nerves when he was working, and this AC/DC song was no exception.

A few minutes later the Pontiac pulled into a Somerville driveway that looked as though it had been paved three-quarters of a century ago and utterly ignored since. Fist-sized chunks of crumbled pavement littered the surface. Deep potholes were randomly scattered along the thirty-foot length, like landmines in a war zone.

Jack drove past and then pulled to a stop in front of a triple-decker tenement building half a block down. He exited quickly as the Pontiac's owner navigated his driveway, moving slowly to avoid dropping into a hole and possibly breaking an axle. The man stopped in front of an ancient garage, constructed with old-fashioned wooden doors that opened outward on hinges, a style that probably hadn't been available since the 1940s.

The target left his car running as he stepped out and slid a key into a padlock securing the two sides of the door. He was unaware of being stalked; his focus was in front of him rather than to the rear.

Jack moved quickly along the sidewalk and then turned ninety degrees and disappeared behind a row of poorly trimmed shrubs. He thought they might be ficus bushes but couldn't be sure. Whatever they were, they provided excellent cover, and in seconds he was less than ten feet from his prey, screened from view and invisible to the man, who was humming to himself as he turned the key.

The padlock clicked smartly and the man removed it from the doors. *Interesting,* Jack thought. *The garage is practically falling down from neglect but the lock is shiny and new. This must be where he stores it.*

The man swung the doors open one by one and then tossed

the padlock casually to the floor just inside the entrance. Then he clomped back to his car, slid behind the wheel, and accelerated into the garage.

As the car eased past the shrubs, Jack pushed his way through, enduring scratches on his bare arms but covering his face with his gloved hands. He slipped through the still-open garage doors as the Le Mans was jerking to a stop.

The driver killed the engine and climbed out of his car, whistling softly now. Jack stood unmoving in the shadows, Sig Sauer P226 held loosely in his right hand. For the time being he kept the gun at his side, pointed at wooden floorboards worn smooth by decades of use. The man flipped a switch and weak yellow light filled the interior of the garage, courtesy of a single uncovered bulb mounted in the ceiling.

He still didn't see Jack.

The man walked to the rear of the garage and reached for one of the doors to swing it shut. The moment he turned toward the street, Jack eased out of the corner and moved behind him.

Stopped slightly to the side.

Cleared his throat.

The driver froze. He swiveled his head until he was staring directly into the barrel of Jack's Sig, which was no longer at Jack's side but now held at eye level. Jack hadn't bothered with a sound suppressor. He didn't intend to shoot the man unless left with absolutely no choice. And even if that *was* how this all went down, he knew he'd be able to put two slugs into his prey and then slip out of the garage and disappear long before the cavalry's arrival.

The man's eyes widened, but only slightly. Jack had to give him credit; he was a cool customer. Not that it would make any difference.

Jack smiled and said, "Whaddaya say you pull that other door closed and give us a little privacy?"

"And why would I do that?" The man's voice shook, but almost imperceptibly. A tough guy.

"Because if you don't, they're going to have to scrape your brains off the wall behind you with a putty knife."

The man hesitated a moment longer, clearly liking where this was going less and less. Along about now Jack knew his prey would consider making a play for the gun, and he waited patiently, allowing the doomed man to go through the exercise of calculating his odds of survival.

Then he shook his head, the smile never leaving his face.

"You're not fast enough," he said, and the man's eyes narrowed in fear and frustration.

Then the target turned back toward the street, exactly as Jack had known he would. What choice did he have? He took a step to his left and pulled the door shut, sealing himself into the garage with his fate.

"Good decision," Jack said agreeably.

The man ignored him. Said, "What's this all about? If you're here to rip me off, you'd better turn around right now and get the fuck out. Whatever product you make off with won't be worth the effort. Trust me on this. When my suppliers find out I've been robbed, they'll hunt you down like a dog and take every bit of their loss, and more, out of your sorry ass. They'll cut you up and toss whatever's left of your corpse into Boston Harbor. No one'll ever know what happened to you."

It was obvious the man had practiced his speech many times. Hell, maybe he had even used it once or twice on actual people. His hard-ass act was fairly impressive under the circumstances. It had to be difficult to pull off while staring down the barrel of a lethal weapon.

But it wasn't going to make any difference, impressive or not. The speech meant nothing to Jack, and he stood quietly, letting the target blow off steam.

When the man finally took a breath, Jack said, "Does the name Brett Farnum mean anything to you?"

The target blinked in surprise. It was obvious he had expected some kind of reaction to his threats. It hadn't occurred to him they might simply be ignored. "What are you talking about?" he finally said.

"It's a simple question. Shouldn't take much thought, even for someone with your . . . intellectual limitations. Brett Farnum. Do you recognize the name?"

"No, alright? I don't recognize the fucking name." The man's voice tightened as anger began to overcome his shock and the fear.

"That's surprising, because you killed Brett Farnum three months ago."

"You're outta your fucking mind. I already told you, I never heard of the dude."

"He was younger than you. Just a kid. A recovering heroin addict who'd been clean for a year. When he relapsed, you killed him by selling him black tar cut with strychnine."

Understanding began to dawn in the man's eyes. Then he narrowed his gaze and said, "Jesus Christ, I don't know what you're talking about. You can't prove I sold anyone anything, certainly not beyond a reasonable doubt."

Jack shoved the barrel of his Sig up against the man's forehead, his own anger rising. "Reasonable doubt? Look around, jackass. This look like a courtroom to you? Do I look like an attorney? You want to raise on objection on procedural grounds?"

"Okay, okay," the target said. "Calm down. I get your point, even if I don't quite understand all the words. But here's the thing: I *always* cut heroin with something; it's a necessary part of the procedure, and strychnine is what I normally use. If this Brett guy was an addict, he would have known all that."

"I'll have to take your word on that. We can't ask him, because he's *dead*. But he probably did know all that. What he *didn't* know was that you screwed up and cut the tar with three times the amount of strychnine needed to down an elephant."

The man's eyes began to wander as he realized where the conversation was going. Jack had seen it before—dozens of times. The prey was looking for a way to defend himself as the walls began to close in.

It was time to refocus him. Gain his full attention.

Jack swiveled his wrist and tapped the side of the guy's head with the butt of the Sig. Not hard enough to do any real damage, just a way of reminding the target of his position in the pecking order.

The gun thudded against the man's skull and he gasped in pain. "Pay attention," Jack said. "We were talking about strychnine."

"Yeah, yeah, right, I remember," he said. His eyes were watering and Jack knew he wanted to rub the side of his head but didn't dare lift his hand. "It wasn't me," he said. "Must've been somebody else."

"It *was* you. I found Brett's street dealer and with just a little of the proper motivation—it didn't take much at all, I might add; you guys abandon a sinking ship faster than rats on the Titanic—he pointed me to you. He gets his entire supply from you, as do dozens of other small-time dealers in the area. And he doesn't do a thing to the heroin. He doesn't even open the baggies. He just sells it as he gets it. Therefore, you killed Brett Farnum."

"Listen," the dealer said, lowering his voice conspiratorially, as if suddenly concerned someone might overhear. "I've got plenty of cash. Give me a few minutes to get it together and it's all yours if you agree to walk away now and forget about the whole thing. I mean, it's one fucking junkie. Who really gives a shit, am I right?"

Jack felt his hand tightening on the butt of the Sig and had to force himself not to slip his finger onto the trigger and keep squeezing. It would be so easy—and so satisfying—to do.

Instead, he took a deep breath and said, "Who gives a shit? His mother, that's who gives a shit. She tells me Brett worked like a dog to break free of his addiction, and slimeballs like you kept hounding him until you pulled him back in, just to make a buck. You sicken me, but more importantly, you sicken her. You took away one mother's only reason for living. And now you're going to get what you have coming to you."

"But—"

"Don't bother trying again with the money offer. I don't care how much cash you have. I don't want it. I'm here to get justice for one woman that can't get it any other way, and that's what I'm going to do."

"So you're just going to shoot me in cold blood."

Jack smiled thinly. "As much as I'd love to do just that, the answer is, no, I'm not going to shoot you. Unless, of course, you force me to. I have something special planned for you, courtesy of one broken-hearted mother."

"What are you talking about?" The dealer's fear was starting to spike. Jack could hear it in his words, the way his voice wavered. The way he started to speak faster, desperate for a way out of the fix he so unexpectedly found himself in.

Jack ignored the question and nodded at the man's right hand. His car keys were still clenched in his fist. "Very slowly, hand me your keys."

The man glanced down as if he had forgotten all about them. Probably he had. Jack could see him weighing the possibility of slashing at his face with them and said quietly, "Don't even think about it."

The man huffed and reluctantly handed Jack his keys.

"Very good. Now, turn around and get back in your car."

"Where are we going?"

"Just do it." Jack prodded him again with the gun, another little tap, and the dealer trudged reluctantly across the ancient garage. He hesitated at his car and then opened the door.

Jack slipped his body between the dealer and the car door so the increasingly desperate man couldn't slam it closed and lock it. His doing so wouldn't have made a difference ultimately, but shooting through a car window would have complicated matters and made things unnecessarily messy. Not to mention noisy.

The man slipped into the driver's seat as Jack was reaching into his back pocket with his left hand. His right kept the Sig trained steadily on the dealer. The moment the man's ass hit his seat, Jack slapped one bracelet of a pair of handcuffs around his left wrist, then tapped the butt of his weapon against the man's skull again, this time using a little more force.

The dealer grunted in pain and surprise and his head lolled to the side. His eyes glazed over and he blinked rapidly. Before he could recover his senses, Jack placed his weapon on the roof of the car and leaned inside, threading the cuffs through the steering column and then snapping the second bracelet around the man's other wrist.

The target groaned and shook his head. Jack bent and reached under the driver's seat, felt around for a moment, and then pulled out a Ruger SR22 semiautomatic pistol. Undoubtedly the dealer had more surprises stashed around the interior of the garage.

He examined the weapon for a moment with a critical eye and then ejected the magazine and tossed it into the back seat. The car was a mess of empty fast-food bags and wrappers, dirty clothing and assorted other detritus of a man too slovenly to keep his vehicle clean. The magazine landed on top of a pile of junk and then disappeared under a pair of stained gym shorts.

The now-useless Ruger he threw onto the passenger side floor.

It bounced off a half-full water bottle, clunking into the door and falling onto the frayed floor mat.

Then he waited for the glaze of pain and confusion to fade in the dealer's eyes. After a moment the man breathed out explosively, muttered, "Goddamn it," and turned his head and locked eyes with Jack.

"You'll notice," Jack said without preamble, "that you're now chained inside your car. You'll also notice that I've disabled your gun. I don't doubt you have other weapons in here somewhere. At least two, unless I've misjudged you."

He stared into the dealer's eyes. Without thinking, the man glanced across the garage and then tried to look away nonchalantly. Jack smiled and said, "Ah, okay, one then. As I was saying, you have one more weapon hidden in here somewhere."

The man jerked as if Jack had hit him in the head with his gun again and then sighed deeply.

Jack shrugged and said in response, "Lucky guess. Anyway, the point is that you've been defanged. You're at my mercy, are we clear about that?"

The man refused to answer and Jack continued. "I've got a couple of things to do before we bring this little visit to a close, but I feel it's only fair to warn you: if you try to draw anyone's attention by blowing your car's horn, I'll come back here and shoot you in the head. If you yell or scream or do anything else to upset me any more than I already am, I'll come back here and shoot you in the head. Do you see the common theme here?"

Jack didn't expect an answer, but the man surprised him by grunting, "What difference does it make? You're going to kill me anyway."

"Did I say that? I don't remember saying that. All I told you was that you were going to get what was coming to you."

The dealer narrowed his eyes and Jack walked away, leaving him now thoroughly confused as well as afraid and bleeding from the head. He strolled to the front of the garage where a workbench had been set up. The top of the workspace was immaculate and completely clear, covered with doctor's office examining room paper. The paper hung on a holder bolted to one wall and could be pulled like a roll of paper towels and then draped over the table to provide a clean work environment.

Beneath the table a series of plastic bins had been stacked on top of one another. Jack glanced back through the windshield at the dealer, who was now glowering at him through hooded eyes. Then he crouched down and began checking the contents of the bins, digging through them with gloved hands.

Bingo.

Bricks of heroin and assorted measuring devices and cutting supplies filled the bins. Jack was amazed at the arrogance of the dealer, who had not taken any measures to secure the area besides locking the garage. The possibility of robbery obviously didn't concern him, but the potential for tragedy was immense. If a neighborhood kid happened to break in here on a lark, as neighborhood kids of a certain age everywhere had a tendency to do, the result could be at least one dead teenager and potentially many more.

Again Jack's blood pressure began to rise. A headache was forming at the base of his skull. It wasn't enough that this idiot was contributing to the deaths of people caught in the grip of addiction; any twelve year old with a crowbar and a curious disposition could easily be victimized, too.

It was time to finish this.

Jack opened one bin after another, leaving the covers strewn about the garage floor, until he found what he was looking for: processed heroin, ready for distribution from this dealer to his street team. Glassine bag after glassine bag, filled with powder and sealed with twist-ties, had been stacked next to small plastic syringes like those used by diabetics, capped off and ready for use.

Full service, Jack thought, and curled his lip. He had collected his usual fee from Mr. Stanton after agreeing to take on this job, but decided right here and now to return it upon completion, to be refunded in full to Brett Farnum's grieving mother.

This assignment would be on the house.

Jack picked up a baggie and examined the contents, wondering how many other addicts had been killed by the abnormally high level of strychnine in the batch of heroin that had been supplied to Brett Farnum. It had undoubtedly long since disappeared in the three months that had elapsed since Farnum's death, but Jack wasn't worried. He could always improvise. It was a particular talent of his.

He pulled three baggies of heroin out of the bin and dropped them onto the workspace. Then he lifted out a syringe and placed it next to the heroin. Returned to the bin filled with cutting supplies and removed a small metal canister, slightly larger and deeper than a big spoon, which he placed next to the other items on the examination paper, everything lined up in a neat, precise row.

Then he stood and stretched.

Thought for a moment.

"I need a little water," he muttered to himself.

He remembered tossing the empty Walther into the passenger side of the dealer's messy car. It had bounced off a partly full water bottle before coming to rest on the floor. That would do perfectly, assuming it actually contained water and not vodka or gin or who knew what else.

Jack walked around the car and opened the door. Picked up the water bottle and examined the contents. Unscrewed the cap and sniffed. Then he shrugged and looked at his prisoner. "This contain water?" he asked.

The man ignored his question, but he had been watching Jack closely the entire time and his wide-eyed gaze and increased agitation told Jack he had finally tumbled to what was coming. "I don't touch that shit," he said, the words coming out in a rush and making him sound breathless. "I'm not a user, so don't even think about it."

Jack had known this moment was coming and was a little surprised it had taken this long for it to arrive. On the other hand, anyone who would leave tens of thousands of dollars in illegal drugs inside a garage protected by a single padlock couldn't be considered a criminal mastermind under any circumstances.

He began walking around the car, holding the dealer's gaze as he went. "I don't blame you for not using," he said. "Dangerous, right?"

The man ignored his comment and kept babbling, and Jack continued. "It was especially dangerous for Brett Farnum."

By now he had reached the dealer's door. He leaned inside the car and unbuckled the man's belt, yanking it off the waistband of his jeans. He reached into the back seat and lifted the dirty gym shorts, wrinkling his nose with distaste.

Moving quickly, he stuffed the shorts into the dealer's mouth as the man was repeating the offer of cash that Jack had already rebuffed once. Apparently he was out of original ideas. Jack looped the belt around the man's head and then pulled it tight, anchoring the shorts in place and cutting off the flood of words mid-bribe.

Then he returned to the workbench. He slit open one of the bags of heroin and dumped it into the metal canister. Poured some of the water over the powder. Reached into his pocket and pulled out a disposable lighter, which he flicked and held under the canister until the concoction inside started bubbling. It didn't take long.

After a moment he placed the canister on top of the workbench and uncapped the syringe. He dipped the needle into the liquid and drew back on the plunger until the syringe was filled.

He walked over to the dealer, who was now bouncing around in his seat like a little boy who had to go to the bathroom. He was trying desperately to speak but could manage nothing more than the muffled sounds of panic and terror.

"I know what you're thinking," Jack said. "We need a filter. Unfortunately, we don't have anything to use as one." He shot the dealer a sympathetic look. "We'll just have to make do, I guess. When you think about it, it's not going to matter much, anyway, in the long run."

The man renewed his pointless efforts at escape, thrashing and bucking. By now his actions were so frenzied that Jack thought, if given enough time, Mr. Big Shot Drug Dealer might actually kill himself by heart attack or stroke.

But he wasn't here for *maybes*. He was here to do a job, thoroughly and completely. And time was beginning to become an issue. There was no telling if or when his new friend might have visitors.

He watched for another moment and finally decided he had seen enough. "This won't do," he said, and slugged the dealer in the head one last time with the butt of his Sig. He put most of his muscle behind this blow, and the man moaned and slumped back in his seat, his eyes rolling up into his head.

"I was really hoping you'd be awake to experience this, but we all have our crosses to bear," he said, crouching down on his haunches and examining the crook of the man's left arm. It was clean, meaning the dealer had been telling the truth about not being a heroin user.

Or maybe he really was a user and he injected somewhere else on his body. It was a possibility.

Not that it mattered.

Jack slapped the skin hard a few times and a greenish-purple vein rose up. He nodded grimly and placed the tip of the syringe against the skin. Then he gently inserted the needle into the vein and eased the plunger down until the contents of the syringe had been expelled into the dealer's arm.

The unconscious man stirred, moaning behind his gag. His arms and legs twitched but he did not awaken. Jack waited a moment and then moved to the workbench and repeated the procedure.

Twice.

When he had finished, he checked the man's pulse. It was rapid and erratic. His skin was much paler than it had been upon Jack's arrival, and sweat glistened on his forehead.

He would be dead within minutes.

Jack stood and gazed at the drug dealer, not pleased with what he had done but not upset, either.

It was his job.

And he was good at his job.

He waited a moment longer and then he slipped out the garage door, not bothering to lock it behind him, not even bothering to close it. There was no reason to. As soon as he had gotten into his rental car and driven a couple of blocks, he would notify the police of the dead man via burner phone before tossing the device into a trash barrel.

Involving the authorities certainly wasn't standard procedure, but nothing about this assignment had been standard. Jack couldn't take the chance of someone finding the heroin and whatever the hell else the dealer had hidden inside his garage and/or his house. It was imperative the drugs get taken off the street immediately.

He drove slowly back to where he had waited an hour or so ago for the dealer, then pulled to the curb.

Called the Somerville police and left an anonymous tip.

Drove to Logan Airport and returned the rental car.

Then he climbed into his truck and headed for Southern New Hampshire and home.

2

Joel Stark pulled his car into a rest stop somewhere along I-80 in Ohio. He didn't know exactly *where* in Ohio he was because it didn't matter. He had been on the road a long time, though, and that *did* matter. His ass hurt and he was dog-tired and he could almost feel his back stiffening by the minute.

Plus, he needed gas and he had to pee. So when he saw the sign for the traveler's plaza, he aimed for the off-ramp and paid no attention to mile markers or town names or anything else. He'd take a short break and then get back on the road. His goal was to get to Las Vegas as quickly as possible and that was what he was going to do. Whether he was in Ashtabula, Akron or Dayton was irrelevant.

Joel Stark was nothing if not single-minded.

He had pulled out of Brooklyn with a full tank of gas and evil intent at seven-thirty this morning, knowing he would face brutal rush-hour traffic getting out of the city but accepting the inevitable delays. They would be worth the aggravation. Once the congestion cleared, he would at least be farther along than he would have been had he slept in and departed later, and who needed sleep, anyway?

Single-minded.

It was now nearly nine-thirty on a clear, cool night. He had been driving for virtually fourteen hours straight, stopping only every few hours, and only for a few minutes at a time to refuel, piss, grab a burger or sandwich, and then hit the road again. He had covered almost eight hundred miles of his journey, an impressive feat given the amount of traffic he had faced early in the day.

He eased into a parking spot outside a utilitarian-looking brick and glass building, shut off his engine and stepped onto the tarmac. Stretched and checked out his surroundings. Eighteen-wheel behemoths dominated the lot, outnumbering passenger vehicles like Joel's by at least a three-to-one margin.

He shivered in the slight chill of the late-spring air as he locked his car and turned toward the restaurant. Out on the interstate, passing vehicles created an endless symphony of road noise. The constant whine of rubber on asphalt was irritating, like a mosquito buzzing around his head, and he tried to ignore it.

The cafeteria-style restaurant was tired-looking and plain and seemed as though it had been lifted straight out of the 1950s and plunked down in the middle of nowhere in the middle of the 2010s. The girl at the cash register was probably nineteen or twenty, average-looking but with a sort of resigned desperation written all over her face, like the thought of doing this job for the next five or six decades was almost too much to bear but she knew she stood no chance of ever getting out of Bumfuck, Ohio.

She was nothing compared to the girl who haunted Joel's dreams every night and most of every day. But just by virtue of her sex she reminded him of the reason he was making this long-distance trek.

Joel dragged his plastic tray along a stainless steel track, passing in front of macaroni and cheese, mashed potatoes, gray meat loaf and unidentifiable other food items that looked as though they had stopped being fresh about the time Joel was getting his driver's license. He stopped in front of a grilling station, and the girl trudged down the line to meet him with an expression on her face that said she would rather be almost anywhere else, doing almost anything else except serving him.

"Help ya?" she asked, indifference oozing out of every pore in her body.

He said nothing, staring at the girl's chest and making absolutely no effort to hide his interest in it. Her uniform buttons strained to hold her breasts captive. The young woman might be a plain Jane, but she had great tits; Joel had to give her that. The blouse was a little too small, and when the girl turned to her right, he could see a hint of red lacy bra peeking through the openings between the buttons.

She was delectable.

* * *

Jessica Trapp's face flushed bright red. She could feel it happening but was powerless to stop it.

After a whole year spent working in this dump, having started the week after high school graduation, she would have thought she'd be used to the lecherous stares and clumsy come-ons from the endless supply of truck drivers and perverted weirdos who seemed drawn to this place on the overnight shift. But every time she felt a strange man's gaze running over her body, she reacted exactly the same way. She felt dirty and wished she could take a shower.

"Sir?" she said again. "What would you like?" The creepy bastard's wolfish smile widened and she immediately regretted her unfortunate choice of words.

He finally raised his eyes from her chest to her face, and when he did she had to suppress an urge to shudder. The man's eyes were flat. Lifeless. Reptilian.

Jessica immediately glanced around the dining room to see if there was anyone who might be able to help her when the trouble started. A couple of truckers way down at the back of the room, sharing a table as they falsified their logbooks. An elderly couple. That was about it.

Maybe the truckers would step up if she needed help; there was no way of knowing until it happened.

When she looked back at the man's face, she again found him staring at her breasts. The intensity of his gaze would have been comical if it weren't so damned frightening. Finally, and to her immense relief, the guy said, "Cheeseburger and fries" in a strangely toneless voice.

She turned to slap the burger onto the grill and felt the man's eyes crawling all over her ass like ants on a picnic lunch. The meat sizzled and popped and Jessica walked as casually as she could into the kitchen for no other reason than to escape those awful shark eyes.

The night manager was a large, matronly silver-haired woman named Georgie. She'd been working at the traveler's plaza since before Jessica was born. Breathlessly, Jessica whispered, "Georgie, you wouldn't believe the creep out there!"

The older woman looked up from the mountain of potatoes she was peeling. "Only one? Well, that's an improvement, wouldn't you say?"

Jessica tried to smile at her boss's joke and it felt forced, fake. "No, I'm serious. It's like *The Walking Dead* out there. I think he's a zombie or something."

"Well, get out there and serve him before he decides to kill us and eat our brains."

She could feel the color drain from her face and the manager said, "I'm just funnin' ya. Probably."

Jessica took a deep breath and said, "Okay. Yeah. Right," her voice shaking just a bit. She knew she was being silly but she couldn't help it; the guy was that creepy.

Finally she turned around and reversed course to the grill, flipping the burger and wishing desperately it would finish cooking so she could get this scary dude on his way. He didn't appear to have moved an inch while she was in the kitchen.

After an eternity the burger was done. She passed it over the counter and dared to take a closer look at him. Greasy brown hair—curly, but not "cute" curly, just "gross" curly—hung limply over a face pocked by the remains of adolescent acne scarring. A pair of soulless, empty eyes glowed black above a mashed nose that had obviously been broken at least once.

This time Jessica did shudder; she couldn't help it. She hoped their hands wouldn't touch as she handed him his food. They didn't and she was glad.

Despite her fears, there was no trouble. The man moved to the register with his tray, paid for his food, and then turned and walked into the dining room. Her sense of relief was overwhelming. Jessica had nearly been raped once as a high school freshman while out on a date with a senior boy, and at the end of that night she had felt frightened but also angry as hell.

This man just left her frightened.

*   *   *

Joel Stark ate his food alone and in silence. He had enjoyed putting a scare into the little slut at the counter. Her fear had been written all over her homely face. It was exhilarating and an incredible turn-on.

He had been half-tempted to shout, "Boo!" as he was paying for his meal, just to see if he could get her to piss her pants. He was pretty sure he could have. But as much fun as that would have been, it was important he keep his eye on the ball and remember why he was out here in the middle of Nowhereville, Ohio to begin with.

And screwing with some hick farm girl wasn't the reason.

He finished his burger and then went to the men's room to take a leak. Looked behind the counter for his new girlfriend as he walked and was unsurprised to see that she had abandoned her station. Joel guessed it would take a kitchen fire to get her back out to the dining room while he was still here, and he smiled thinly. Sometimes life's little pleasures were the best.

He found himself whistling softly as he crossed the massive parking lot to his car. He started it up and drove the short distance to the gas station conveniently located between the restaurant and the interstate on-ramp.

Then he filled the tank and hit the road again. He still had a long way to go, and his best girl was waiting for him at the end of the journey.

3

Rudy Palermo had the look of a banker, bland and anonymous. He was average height for a man, average weight as well. Brown hair, brown eyes. Glasses prescribed to combat a mild astigmatism. Dressed in a suit, as he usually was, he looked exactly like a thousand other guys dressed in suits.

Anonymous.

And that was good. Anonymity allowed him to blend into crowds, to become—or remain—invisible, to perform his duties as a made member of Vegas's Mercadante crime family without ever becoming memorable in the eyes of potential witnesses. For a mob guy who was expected to get his hands dirty—and sometimes bloody—every now and then, being memorable would not have been conducive to a long career.

Rudy's assignment today was a touchy one. He knew that in all likelihood it would end in bloodshed somewhere down the line, and while he had no problem with that—he relished the opportunity to pull the trigger in this case, if he was being honest with himself—he appreciated his "regular-guy" persona even more than usual today because of that possibility.

He was tasked with tailing a man he knew very well. In fact, it was a fellow member of the Mercadante family, albeit a man much lower on the company ladder. The man was a jack-of-all-trades, a courier/enforcer with the improbably exotic name of Blake Arthur Standiford III. Standiford, who Rudy detested with a passion normally reserved for people who owed him large sums of money and were late with their payments, was rumored to be sleeping with the wrong woman.

The wrongest possible woman.

Incredibly, Blake Arthur Standiford III—if persistent rumors were to be believed—was screwing Kathleen Saldana, wife of Shotgun Sammy Saldana, the longtime leader of one of LA's most violent crime families. The Saldana crowd was bad-tempered and ambitious, moving quickly up the rungs of the Southern California crime scene by extorting, blackmailing, and murdering anyone in their way, including—and especially—the strategically important people in rival gangs.

Thus far, the Saldanas had limited the expansion of their territory to the LA basin, but Rudy knew that if Big Tony Mercadante's information about Standiford and Kathy Saldana getting horizontal was anything close to accurate, that situation would likely change. Saldana would train his murderous gaze on Las Vegas.

And quickly.

And blood would flow. Lots of it.

In addition to the obvious problem of having to fight off the Saldanas when Shotgun Sammy learned of his wife's affair—and he *would* learn of it eventually—there was the issue of whether Standiford was sharing Mercadante family secrets, and which ones, if he was. Pillow talk was always dangerous, but never more so than when the person sharing the pillow was connected to thugs possessing the firepower and the will to cut you down and bury your bullet-riddled body in the desert if they so chose.

Big Tony had told Standiford two weeks ago in no uncertain terms to dump the Saldana bitch, and Standiford had responded in his inimitable fashion: by denying any affair, and then agreeing in the next breath that if he *had* been seeing Kathy Saldana—not that he was, you understand—he would, of course, immediately break off the affair.

Big Tony confided to Rudy at the time that he didn't believe Standiford had it in him to quit Shotgun Sammy's wife, and now, after several reported sightings of the two together—right here in Vegas, no less—Tony had had enough. He hated being ignored almost as much as he hated the idea of a war with the Saldana family, so this morning he had called Rudy into his office. Unlit cigar stuck into his mouth like a movie prop, Big Tony had said, "I want you to follow that stupid horny bastard for as long as it takes to determine one way or the other whether he's really enough of an asshole to ignore my orders and continue screwing Shotgun Sammy's wife."

Rudy nodded. "I can do that."

"Don't let him outta your sight. If he takes a crap, get into the stall next to him. If he goes to the dentist, get in the goddamn chair with him, understand?"

So here was Rudy, sitting in the casino at the Luxor, playing blackjack without looking at his cards. It was mid-morning and the place was maybe two-thirds full, a decent crowd considering the early hour. Most of the gamblers consisted of young couples honeymooning and old geezers blowing their grandkids' inheritance.

A short distance across the casino, more or less screened by the constant flow of gamblers moving across the floor, sat Blake Standiford, the Stupid Horny Bastard himself. Standiford also was playing blackjack while barely paying attention to his cards.

Rudy wouldn't have been worried about Standiford spotting him even if there weren't a moving wall of people between them, because Blake seemed to have eyes for only one thing: the chick standing next to him. She was long and willowy, and as he played he watched her with the intense concentration of a vulture circling a carcass in the desert.

It was Kathy Saldana.

Holy shit, stop the presses, the rumors really were true.

Rudy could kind of understand Blake screwing Saldana, at least a little. She was no kid; that much was true. But she was a lot younger than Shotgun Sammy and looked as though she could be a gracefully aging lingerie model. Heidi Klum, say, if Heidi were to put on about fifteen pounds and wrinkle up a little.

And Blake Standiford was nothing more than a low-level scumbag, paid handsomely to break bones and occasionally put people underground in places their corpses would never be found. He was an enforcer and it was all he would ever be, despite his grand illusions to the contrary.

So his interest in the wife of a mob boss made a certain amount of sense. Why Kathy Saldana would care about a cockroach like Blake Standiford was another question entirely, one Rudy knew he would likely never be able to answer. No accounting for taste, and all that.

What he didn't understand was how Blake could be so monumentally stupid as to agree, in front of their boss and God Himself, which in the Mercadante family was almost the same thing, to stop seeing the Saldana bitch and then simply flaunt their continued relationship right here in Vegas.

Prior to this morning Rudy wouldn't have believed even Standiford could be that brazen. Did he think Big Tony wouldn't find out? Could he really be *that stupid?* Why didn't he just pay for an ad on a Hollywood billboard while he was at it? "Hey Sammy, you old coot, I'm having a great time in Vegas doing your wife! Sincerely, Blake Arthur Standiford III, AKA The Stupid Horny Bastard."

Maybe he could add a candid photo of some hot bedroom action, too, the kinkier the better, just on the off-chance Sammy wouldn't be pissed off enough when he found out.

Rudy shook his head. His dislike for Standiford bordered on the obsessive, maybe because Blake Arthur was everything he, Rudy, was not. Standiford was tall, blond and handsome and looked like an extra in a 1960s surfer movie. He carried himself with a confidence bordering on arrogance, like he knew every woman's eyes were on him when he walked into a room.

The worst part was that it was true: most of the time women *were* admiring his chiseled body and square-jawed good looks. It was only after you talked to the guy for a while—and usually a short while—did it begin to become clear he was about as bright as a bag of hammers.

Rudy wondered idly whether The Stupid Horny Bastard would seem as attractive to women when he was sporting a big, ugly bullet hole in his forehead. Because he had a strong suspicion that would be the eventual result of Rudy's report to Big Tony.

He kept an eye on the unlikely couple while entertaining himself with pleasant fantasies of being the one to pull the trigger on Standiford. Eventually, the lovesick idiot rose and began threading his way through the crowd. Saldana followed a short distance behind him. There was no arm-in-arm stuff, no hand-holding, nothing at all to indicate to a casual observer that they were together.

But Rudy Palermo was no casual observer. He tossed in his losing hand and ambled along behind them, curious about what would happen next although he thought he had a pretty good idea. Shotgun Sammy kept a second-floor room permanently rented in the Luxor for use when he was in Vegas, and Standiford was heading straight for the staircase, Kathy Saldana still trailing along behind him like an Italian sports car drafting behind a Mack truck.

Rudy whistled softly through his teeth. The Stupid Horny Bastard had balls, he had to give him that. Big brass ones.

The crowd thinned as the pair left the casino, and Rudy was forced to drop a little farther behind. He still had a clear view, though, as Saldana caught up with Standiford in the hallway. Blake turned and reached for her hand and she flinched, pulling it away but drawing close to him.

That was odd, Rudy thought. He watched from the end of the hallway as Kathy Saldana swiped her key card and the pair entered the room of one of the most dangerous men in LA. The door thunked closed behind them and even from the end of the hallway Rudy could hear the locks click.

He chuckled darkly. This was one of the most bizarre things he had ever seen and after a lifetime spent in Vegas that was saying something. It was ten- thirty a.m., less than two hours into his surveillance, and he had already dug up the proof his boss had requested. Big Tony was not going to like this. Not one little bit.

For a moment, Rudy felt a stab of sympathy for Blake Arthur Standiford III.

But just for a moment.

And then it was gone.

4

When Big Tony told him to stop seeing Shotgun Sammy Saldana's wife, Blake had known immediately that was not going to happen.

He wasn't an idiot, though. His continued employment in the Mercadante family represented the key to everything Blake wanted. Namely, money.

In this career field, Blake raked in more cash every week than he had ever dreamed possible while growing up a petty thief and drug dealer, and he had been working for Big Tony Mercadante for years. His job description was no more complicated than doing what he was naturally predisposed toward, anyway: intimidating, bullying and hurting people.

And occasionally killing them.

So while he had zero respect for Big Tony, he wasn't quite prepared to blow the guy off, either. At least not yet.

And he didn't have to. He simply lied through his teeth. He stood in front of Tony's desk and agreed to stop seeing Kathy Saldana.

It was easy. Blake had been lying, cheating and manipulating his way through life practically from the day he spoke his first words, and he had no compunction whatsoever about doing exactly that to his boss.

Because actually going through with it and cutting Shotgun Sammy's wife loose was more than he could manage. It was more than he *wanted* to manage. Kathy was tall and leggy, with big tits, almost but not quite beautiful, and incredibly well preserved for a broad pushing forty. She was stylish and classy and, best of all, ready and willing and kinky in the bedroom.

Plus, she was *Shotgun Sammy Saldana's wife*, for chrissakes. The perverse rush Blake got out of screwing the wife of one of the most influential mob bosses west of the Mississippi was electric, and not something he was willing to sacrifice just to make Fat Tony's life a little easier.

Hell, if he played his cards right, he wouldn't have to put up with Tony's shit much longer anyway. All he had to do was figure out how to leverage his secret relationship with Kathy into a spot on Sammy's team. Blake thought he'd enjoy living in LA, and he wasn't above blackmailing or threatening Kathy Saldana to make it happen.

In the meantime, though, he was determined to continue nailing this babe, with or without Tony Mercadante's approval. He'd just have to be a little more careful about it. The stupid bitch showing up as he was relaxing in the casino downstairs wasn't part of the plan; he hadn't even known she was in town.

But what the hell. Blake had looked up and spotted her and his initial burst of anger at the position she was putting him in with Tony had faded almost immediately, replaced by a carnal desire that was almost overwhelming in its intensity. Kathy was dressed down today, in a simple pair of tight blue jeans and a light V-neck sweater. He could see right away she wasn't wearing a bra and he smiled appreciatively.

After keeping her waiting a few minutes—*ya gotta let 'em know who's in charge*—Blake rose from the table and sauntered away without so much as a glance in his lover's direction. She followed immediately, as he had known she would, and caught up with him on the stairs, both of them making a beeline for Sammy's permanent room.

"Blake, we have to talk," Kathy said in her sexy, breathy voice. He loved her voice; she always sounded like she had just gotten laid and couldn't quite catch her breath.

"We can talk when we're done," he said, not even looking at her.

"No, we'll talk *now*." Kathy reached past Blake and slid her key card into the lock. Pushed the door open. Walked into the room and turned to face Blake, whose anger immediately flared. Impulse control was not Blake Standiford's strong suit, and being mouthed at by some little bitch, sexy or not, wife of Sammy Saldana or not, wasn't something he was prepared to take lying down.

Or at all.

He closed and locked the door and then advanced on her. He wrapped his arms around the small of her back, grasping her delectable ass and pulling her body tight against his. The movements were angry and violent, not soft and sensual. The fury rising in Blake mixed with his desire and exploded. He wanted her now and he would have her now.

"Blake, stop it!" Kathy Saldana demanded. She pushed against his chest trying to reestablish some distance between them but was much too weak to accomplish anything against Blake's superior bulk and muscle. "Just listen to me! I've decided I need to spend more time with Sam. He's older. His health is failing. He needs me. You and I are going to have to stop seeing each other. There's no future for us."

Blake gazed flatly at Kathy, the blood rushing in his temples as his pulse pounded inside his skull. Her eyes widened. Blake could tell she was trying to keep her cool but her fear was obvious.

"I'm sorry to break it to you like this," she said, "but I thought I should do it face to face. I thought I owed you that much." Her voice wavered just a little.

Blake heard the words she was saying, but they didn't make any sense. *She* was dumping *him?* And not just dumping him, she was leaving him for some ancient limp-dick liver-spotted walking-dead old bastard?

"Bullshit," he said quietly, the words barely more than a whisper. "Bull fucking shit." No little bitch was going to give him the brushoff, especially not some forty-year-old glorified truck stop whore who had managed to hit the jackpot by sucking off Sammy Saldana so well the crazy old coot had married her.

Blake had released his hold on Kathy out of sheer surprise, and now the two stood facing each other, inches apart. He could feel a vein pulsing in his forehead. He thought his skull might be about to explode. He flexed his fists, one after the other: right, left, right, left.

"How about one last ride then. You know, for old time's sake."
The words came out flat, monotone, deadly.

"I don't think that's a good idea, Blake."

"I don't think that's a good idea, Blake," he mimicked, his
falsetto cracking with rage. "I don't give a *fuck* what you think is a
good idea!"

The pulsing in Blake's forehead had insinuated itself into his
eyeballs, and the room was tinted with a red hue that shifted and
rolled as if alive. He grabbed Kathy by the neck and threw her
across the room. It took barely any effort at all.

She smashed face-first into a wall mirror and it shattered. Then
she staggered backward and fell, knocking a lamp off the night-
stand as she crumpled to the floor. Blood from a dozen gashes ran
down her face.

"Please," she whimpered. "Please stop. Please."

Blake advanced on her, lost in his rage, his limited self-control
long gone. The fists that had beaten so many men and more than
a few women now rained down on Kathy Saldana. He was strong
and in shape and utterly unopposed to using his size and strength
to terrorize his girlfriend.

Correction: ex-girlfriend.

The storm continued until the woman lay dead on the floor, her
battered face virtually unrecognizable.

* * *

Rudy waited half a minute after the door slammed closed before
moving from the end of the hallway. Once he heard the locks
engage he wasn't concerned about Blake leaving the room any
time soon, but just as the pair disappeared into Sammy's room,
an elderly couple appeared farther down the hallway and walked
slowly in his direction.

He waited for the geezers to pass and then eased down the
plush carpet, coming to a stop outside the room The Stupid Horny
Bastard had just entered with his girl. There wasn't anything in
particular to be gained by snooping; Rudy had already gotten the

verification Big Tony wanted. And besides, the rooms in the Luxor were well insulated for privacy, so the occupants would have to be screaming at each other for him to hear anything at all.

Still, he investigated further, anyway.

Rudy slowed to a stop outside Shotgun Sammy's room and was surprised to find that he actually *could* hear something happening on the other side of the door. And it wasn't anything like what he had been expecting. He heard a guttural growl as Standiford shouted, "I don't give a *fuck* what you think is a good idea!"

An instant later he heard a crash and a scream. Rudy couldn't imagine what might have happened in the last sixty seconds to set off The Stupid Horny Bastard, but knowing what he did about Blake Arthur Standiford III and his incredible disappearing self-control, he guessed Kathy Saldana was in big trouble.

And just like that, so was the Mercadante crime family.

5

"Are you shitting me? He was out in public with her? Where anyone could see?" Big Tony was already working himself into a fine froth, and Rudy had been in the boss's office less than thirty seconds. The nickname "Big Tony" was appropriate and in this case well earned. Nobody in the Mecadante family knew for sure how much the man weighed, but everyone agreed it was well north of three hundred pounds, and when Tony got angry, he somehow looked even bigger, like a startled cat puffing out its fur.

Big Tony had a tendency to spit when he got upset. Rudy answered, "Yeah. At the Luxor," while taking what he hoped was an inconspicuously small step backward. He wondered if he was out of range and wished he could have worn rain gear.

"And it gets worse," he continued, doing his best to ignore the sudden light drizzle in the room.

"What the hell could be worse than that?"

"They went into Shotgun Sammy's room and closed the door, so I eased up to it and listened. They were having some kind of altercation. It was physical. You know how that idiot Blake gets when he loses it. I'm afraid he might have killed her."

Tony's eyes bulged out of his head and his faced flushed bright red and he shouted, "Killed her! Are you fucking kidding me?"

The boss wasn't really looking for an answer to that question, Rudy knew, so he kept his mouth shut and waited.

"Jesus Christ," Tony finally sputtered. "That fuckin' dumbass has no idea what kind of a position he's putting us in." He swiped the back of one meaty paw across his chin, drying the spittle and clearing the way for the next wave.

"Well, to be honest, he looked like he was contemplating any number of different positions as they entered the room, but I think she might have told him to get lost," Rudy answered.

Big Tony chuckled and a little of his anger seemed to melt away. "Any number of positions. You're a regular Don Rickles, ya know that?"

Rudy allowed himself a little smile and then plowed ahead. "So, when do you want to take him out?" he asked, hoping against hope Big Tony would assign him the task of eliminating Standiford.

"Whoa, slow down there, big fella. Let's just think about this for a few minutes, shall we? Consider all the angles." Big Tony Mercadante had some anger issues, but he had been on top of the Vegas family for a long time and Rudy knew there was a shrewd, calculating brain under all the brawn and bluster.

Tony propped one elbow on his desk and rested his head in his hand. He stroked the stubble on his chin while he mapped out his options. "There's no question now that we gotta do him, especially if you're right and he killed Sammy's broad. But I'm thinking . . ."

"Yeah?" Rudy was genuinely curious now. It wasn't like Big Tony to be squeamish.

"I'm thinking it might be best if we farm this one out. If we hit Blake ourselves, it will just draw attention to the fact that he's our guy. The wrong people will naturally wonder why we had to do him, and wondering about that could bring his foolishness with the little bitch to Sammy's attention, and that's what we want to avoid. Sammy's old and decrepit, but he ain't stupid. He can still put two and two together, and he's gonna wonder what Kathy was doing—or *who* she was doing—in Vegas in the first place. But if we stay away from the dirty work and get a little lucky, maybe Sammy'll never know for sure it was one of our guys that killed his wife."

Rudy shook his head doubtfully. "I don't know. Blake's been flashing her around town like a fucking diamond ring. The minute Sammy hears she's dead and starts sniffing around, Standiford's name is bound to come up. It might be better to show the old bastard that we took care of business. Maybe that'll mean something to him."

"We can always convince Sammy we contracted the hit afterward if we have to. But you never know how deep Sammy's going to dig. Maybe he was tired of the old ball and chain anyway and ain't really going to be too concerned *who* killed her. But regardless, I think we need to stay as far away from Standiford as we can, at least until we can see which way the wind's blowing with Shotgun Sammy."

Rudy started to speak and Tony continued, almost as if talking to himself. He nodded as he spoke. "What we need is for The Stupid Horny Bastard to meet with an accident unrelated to his employment, and the sooner the better. For that to happen, we need to hire an independent contractor."

6

It didn't take long for Jack to hear from Mr. Stanton after completing the job in Somerville. Although books and movies were rife with stories about assassins, the reality was that there weren't very many around, and the number of potential contracts always seemed to exceed the number of specialists competent to carry out those contracts.

Sure, it was distressingly easy to find someone willing to end another person's life in exchange for cash, and often not that much of it. But the ranks of professionals, men and women who approached their work with diligence and treated the taking of life with the respect the calling entailed, were few and far between.

Jack had heard about a guy who operated out of White Plains—a stamp collector, if he recalled correctly—but he had never met the man and didn't think he would ever want to. The essence of survival in his line of work—besides competence—was secrecy, so it wasn't like there were yearly assassin conventions, where you could glad-hand your fellow professional killers and swap war stories at the bar over drinks.

And that was just fine with Jack Sheridan. He wasn't a professional killer because he enjoyed bloodshed or the taking of human life. He had simply fallen into the line of work during his two stints in the Army, where he had served in a unit so secret, so unknown, that its governance didn't even fall under any single branch of the service.

Jack had traveled the world over, spending much of his time on missions in the Middle East. He eliminated radicals in Afghanistan, Pakistan, Iraq, Iran, Saudi Arabia and other countries. Allies or hated enemies of the United States, it made no difference. He had been chosen for recruitment based on his athleticism, his skill utilizing different types of weapons, his average looks and his relentlessly tight-lipped demeanor.

By the time he had mustered out of his secret unit, Jack's reputation as one of most lethal assassins in the U.S. arsenal was cemented forever, not that anyone outside the world of Black Ops could ever know.

After returning to civilian life and making his home in Southern New Hampshire, Jack had floundered. He found work as a truck driver, a grocery store clerk and an apple picker among other jobs, discovering along the way that the traits that had served him so well in Black Ops were not necessarily the ones that tended to be valued in civilian life.

Two years into his Army retirement, he had been approached by a shadowy figure calling himself "Mr. Stanton." The man was of indeterminate age and carried himself with a recognizably military bearing. Mr. Stanton was not his real name, and Jack knew better than to inquire as to what his real name might be.

Mr. Stanton offered Jack a proposition: employment as a contractor working for The Organization, a group whose name would never be more specific than that and whose ranks were made up of a select few men—and women—with Jack's unique and specific skill set.

His job description would be simple. He would eliminate evil people, those whose actions had made them highly dangerous to the population and who for whatever reason—money, connections, status—were considered untouchable by society's traditional arbiters of justice.

"You will have full autonomy on your assignments and total discretion on whether to accept or reject an offered assignment. You may reject any offered assignment for any reason whatsoever and will never be second-guessed," Mr. Stanton had said.

It was not a typical job offer, obviously. Jack was mystified at how the shadowy "Mr. Stanton" had learned of his involvement in the blackest of military Black Ops units when only a handful of people in the defense community were even aware of the unnamed unit's existence.

Obviously the man had some serious connections, and Jack's immediate suspicion was that the U.S. government was somehow involved in the operations of The Organization. His suspicions had never been resolved one way or the other, and ultimately he had decided the answer was irrelevant. This civilian Black Ops unit was just as secret as the military one had been, just as disciplined, just as well funded.

And just as necessary.

Jack had told Mr. Stanton to take a hike after the initial meeting, but the more he thought about it, the more he realized the offer might be just what he needed. He had never found a niche in the civilian world, and the more he watched the TV news, and the more he read newspaper and Internet reports of the savagery a certain percentage of the human race was capable of inflicting on weaker members of the species, the more he realized a group like The Organization—if disciplined and professional—could serve a vital role in modern society.

After days of soul-searching and considering the offer from every conceivable angle, Jack decided that when Mr. Stanton approached him again—and he *would* approach again, Jack had been involved in the world of intelligence operations far too long to think he had seen the last of the man—he would this time accept the job and return to a world he thought he had left behind forever.

Despite the fact that he had wrestled for years with the morality of killing others—or perhaps *because* of that fact—Jack realized that using his unique abilities to help rid society of its most dangerous sociopaths was likely the only way he would ever be able to contribute something tangible to that society.

He knew many would disagree with his stance on morality. He understood that they might be right. But he decided that *he* was comfortable with his part in the career he was about to return to, and that was all anyone could expect out of this life.

That had been eight years ago, and exactly as he had known would happen, a month or so after he reached his decision, Mr. Stanton had once again appeared out of nowhere with the identical job offer.

And Jack had accepted.

He had had good days and bad days in the intervening eight years, but had never had trouble sleeping at night—not due to his career path, anyway—and doubted he ever would. He had seen too much of human nature to doubt the correctness of his decision. In his own odd and admittedly violent way, he was contributing to a safer world.

* * *

Jack had returned three days ago from sending the Boston drug dealer on to whatever fate awaited him in the next life when his cell phone rang early in the evening as he was sitting down to dinner. Only one person had the number to this particular phone, so there was only one person it could be.

He took a deep breath and answered the call.

* * *

To Jack's way of thinking, Logan Airport in East Boston was the perfect location in which to hold a clandestine meeting. Although logic might suggest otherwise—airports, particularly in the post-9/11 world, were typically crawling with law enforcement, federal government types and metal detectors—Jack had found that the constant bustle of activity, the endless streams of travelers talking and shouting and moving about, made blending into the crowd a simple matter for someone who knew what he was doing.

Jack knew what he was doing, as did Mr. Stanton.

Today's rendezvous was to take place at one of the many restaurants scattered throughout Logan's terminal buildings. After careful consideration he had selected a local seafood joint gone national, known for their clam chowder. Jack loved chowder, and felt the drive into the city would be worthwhile whether he accepted today's assignment or not if he could at least avail himself of a bowl.

He arrived a few minutes early. Took a seat and dug into his chowder, knowing Mr. Stanton would slip into the chair across the table from him at exactly ten a.m., their agreed-upon time. Not one minute before and certainly not one minute after.

He was right. The older man eased into his chair with the grace of an aging athlete and Jack glanced at his watch. "Thirty seconds late," he said. "You're slipping."

"Maybe it's time to have that watch cleaned," came the immediate reply. "It's running a little slow."

Jack smiled took another bite.

"Good job in Somerville," Mr. Stanton said, taking a sip of a cup of coffee. He either didn't enjoy seafood or wasn't hungry, because he hadn't bothered to order anything besides the drink.

"Thanks. That guy was a piece of work, even when compared to the subjects of most of your assignments. In fact, I'm forfeiting my fee on this one. Please make sure Mrs. Farnum gets it. I have a feeling she needs the money more than I do."

Mr. Stanton gazed across the table, his eyes giving away nothing. "Of course," he said after a short pause. Then he cleared his throat. "You know, sentimentality is your enemy in this line of work."

Jack nodded. He had considered that very fact three nights ago, had lost sleep over it in fact, wondering what it said about him. Was he getting soft? Losing his edge?

He didn't know, but what he *did* know was that it was an issue for another time. He had forged a bond with a woman he had never met, and was determined the suffering mother receive her money back.

"What do you have for me?" he asked, allowing Mr. Stanton's comment to pass without acknowledgement.

His contact slid a packet across the table. Jack glanced at it briefly and then put it aside unopened. The packet would contain all the details on the proposed assignment, which of course meant that its examination required privacy. When he got home— assuming he accepted the assignment based on the preliminary information—Jack would be expected to remove all of the materials he would need, such as counterfeit licenses, credit cards, and other forms of identification, and then memorize everything else and destroy the documentation.

He tucked the packet next to his chowder and listened as Mr. Stanton gave a brief rundown of the details of the contract. Protocol dictated that Jack be permitted up to two days to decide whether to accept the contract or reject it, but as Stanton sketched out the job, he knew before his contact had even finished speaking that he would accept the assignment.

He listened quietly, sipping his own coffee. When Mr. Stanton indicated he was finished, Jack said, "Really? Blake Arthur Standiford III? That's the guy's name? What parents in their right mind would ever hang that on a kid? Is he a mobster or a college professor?"

Mr. Stanton rarely smiled. For a long time Jack had wondered if he even knew how. But now his thin lips twisted into the barest hint of one as he said, "I can't answer your question about the name. But as far as his occupation is concerned, my information suggests he probably doesn't even know what a college *is,* much less teach at one. But if he is a professor, he won't be one for much longer now, will he?"

7

The frightened girl at the highway rest stop back in Ohio was just a fond memory as Joel Stark continued across the country in his rusting Pontiac Le Mans. The object of his desire, the reason for this trip, was a girl.

A different girl.

His girl.

Joel had been chasing after his girl for a long time. He'd caught up with her more than once, too. But thanks to his single-minded obsession with her, which led to over-aggressiveness and poor decision-making on his part—he wasn't afraid of a little intro-spection; it was the key to self-improvement, after all—he had allowed her to slip through his fingers every time he came within striking distance.

His girl's name was Victoria Welling, and whenever he thought about her—which amounted to probably three dozen times a day—Joel thanked his lucky stars for his father's extensive network of contacts, which had enabled him to track her down again after she had gone scampering off like a terrified rabbit.

Joel's father, John Stark, was a New York City police detective. And he wasn't just any detective, either. "Stark the Narc" was legendary in lowlife circles for becoming extremely influential, not to mention moderately wealthy, through the selective abuse of his position on the NYPD.

John Stark's job was to take down narcotics traffickers and thus rid the city of the scourge of illegal drugs and their associated criminal activity. And to a point, that was exactly what he did.

But he was nothing if not perceptive, and he'd seen the handwriting on the wall early in his career. He could remain a hardworking public servant, compensated poorly and treated with disdain by the public he was paid to serve, or he could leverage his unique position, using it to acquire wealth and influence of his own.

He chose the second option. Stark the Narc had begun shaking down the distributors in his area of jurisdiction, which included some of the meanest streets in Brooklyn.

He didn't worry about the street dealers. To John Stark those guys were nothing more than low-level suckers, taking most of the risk of the unlawful drug trade while reaping few, if any, of the rewards.

Instead, Stark went for the middlemen, shaking down the dealers to gain access to the regional bosses. After that it was a simple matter to negotiate agreements, whereby Stark would ensure that he and his men were looking the other way during the delivery of certain high-priority shipments into the city.

In exchange for sufficient compensation, of course.

It was a win-win for everyone, with the possible exception of the law-abiding citizens of New York. The scam was by no means new, but the elder Stark discovered he was a natural at playing both sides against the middle, doing just enough legitimate work to keep his NYPD superiors happy—or at least satisfied, more or less—while at the same time raking in hundreds of thousands of dollars in illicit, untraceable cash over the course of his career.

Joel Stark, while appreciative of his father's skills, didn't give a damn about the money. It was okay, he supposed, but of far greater significance to him was that network of contacts his father had built, both legitimate and illegitimate. For the right price, Joel had discovered he was able to utilize those resources to track down the object of his obsession—eventually—no matter where she ran off to or how long she had been gone.

But Joel possessed none of the cunning or cleverness of his father. He was a sledgehammer, an object of brute force. He dropped out of high school after ninth grade, becoming involved in petty theft and the occasional small-time drug deal—an ironic outcome, he knew, given his father's chosen occupation. Through sheer luck and John Stark's behind-the-scenes influence, Joel had avoided any serious jail time.

Until the misadventure involving his favorite girl.

Joel cruised along the interstate at a safe, sedate speed—the last thing he wanted to do was draw the attention of the police now that he was so close to achieving his goal—and thought back to the first time he had set eyes on his princess. It had been the most fortunate of lucky breaks for him to have seen her shortly after her arrival in the city. It had been fate.

His much-too-short time with Victoria had spoiled him for any other girl, not that he hadn't sampled plenty. Everything about her was perfect, from her luxurious ringlets of fiery red hair to her tight, slim body. Daydreaming about her never failed to arouse him.

Unfortunately for Joel, he had been apprehended less than a week after their magical night together, and he had cooled his heels in police custody through two trials—even Daddy's influence hadn't been sufficient to secure bail—before finally winning his freedom.

Since his release, he had split his time and energy evenly between two pursuits: searching for his elusive redheaded quarry, and obsessively "introducing" himself sexually to young women of similar build and hair color in a series of unsuccessful attempts to relive the thrill of his night with Victoria.

Every single one of the girls he so carefully selected had proven themselves unworthy, most *so* unworthy that he had been forced to kill them and dump their bodies. Each successive disappointment only served to fuel his desire for the real thing.

And now, finally, after several blown attempts at winning Victoria's affection, he was nearly there.

Because Joel had once again discovered his princess's location.

And this time, he would not fail. He would put everything he had learned from his past attempts to good use.

Joel switched on the radio and sang/rapped along with Eminem as his battered Le Mans entered the Las Vegas city limits. He had never before visited this city of sin and decadence, but had already decided it was the perfect backdrop for everything he had planned

39

for Victoria Welling. He would enjoy her, oh yes he would, but she must also pay for all that she had put him through over the years.

All the suffering.

All the time spent under lock and key, jailed like a common criminal.

He rubbed his eyes and yawned. He was dog-tired but justifiably proud of himself. He had made it from Brooklyn to Vegas in less than three full days. It was an impressive accomplishment made even more so by the fact that his car seemed constantly on the verge of giving up the ghost.

None of that mattered now, however. Joel wheeled into the parking lot of his chosen motel and nosed into the nearest spot. Killed the engine and shuffled into the office. He had selected the Cactus Motel not for its amenities—there didn't seem to be any—but rather for its proximity to his sweetheart's apartment.

That physical closeness was all he cared about. The place could have been a cockroach-infested shithole—and by the looks of the place, it probably was—but as far as Joel was concerned it was the fucking Taj Mahal.

All he needed was a place to lay his head and catch up on his rest, so that he could begin putting his plan in motion. It was well past time he reintroduced himself to Victoria Welling. He couldn't wait to get started.

8

Jack had learned long ago that there was never any shortage of people who wanted someone dead. Never any shortage of people willing to pay someone else to *make* that someone dead, either.

And while many of The Organization's potential assignments were things Jack wouldn't have touched with a twenty-foot pole, that still left plenty that fit his criteria. He knew it was probably the ultimate in self-deception for a hired assassin to claim any sense of morality, but nevertheless that was exactly what Jack did.

He limited the practice of his unique occupation to those in society who fit a set of stringent personal criteria: men and the occasional woman who had demonstrated in no uncertain terms—and usually many times over—that they possessed zero regard for the welfare of other human beings. People like the drug dealer in Somerville Jack had sent on to his ultimate reward a few days ago. Jack hadn't learned the man's name because he hadn't cared to know the man's name.

In his long career dealing with the lowest forms of societal detritus, Jack had learned that the old saw about murders being committed for one of only two reasons—money or sex—was an old saw because it was, in fact, almost always true.

Thus he was utterly unsurprised to find that his latest assignment would take him to Las Vegas, the American shrine dedicated to the pursuit of both money *and* sex. Jack had worked a couple of jobs in Vegas in the past. It seemed unsavory people were forever doing depraved things to other people in that city, thereby dooming themselves to anonymous desert burials.

This latest assignment involved a low-level mobster slated for elimination by his own gangland family thanks to a messy scenario involving sexual indiscretions with the wife of a rival family's head man. That suicidal bout of lunacy had been followed smartly—or, to be more accurate, stupidly—by the woman's brutal murder at her lover's hands.

In an attempt to avoid an all-out gang war, the Vegas family was hoping to distance themselves from the murderous letch in their employ by contracting the hit out rather than performing it themselves. According to Mr. Stanton, their request to The Organization had been for a death that appeared accidental, or at least one that avoided directing any unnecessary attention at them.

When packing for his flight, Jack had not even considered attempting to smuggle a gun aboard the airplane. That would have been risky prior to September 11, 2001 and was simply out of the question now.

But it didn't matter. He wasn't yet sure how he would arrange for the completion of his task—he would have to wait until arriving on-site and accomplishing some research and reconnaissance to figure that out—but if he changed his mind and decided he needed a weapon, acquiring one would be a simple matter. The Organization had contacts in every major city, at least in all of the ones Jack had ever worked, and he knew he could have virtually any firepower he might need in his hands within a matter of hours.

With that in mind, he packed light, as he always did when working. Better to carry a small bag onto the airplane and then buy clothes on-site, destroying or discarding them when the job was done, than to have to wait for checked baggage at the destination and possibly bring evidence of felony murder home in his luggage.

Jack worked at his computer, finalizing travel plans that would take him though an intermediary destination—in this case, Pittsburgh—rather than direct to Las Vegas. Flying through at least one stopover city and sometimes more was a simple way to avoid leaving a direct trail for the authorities to follow, and Jack always planned his travel carefully.

Also critical to an operation's success was the judicious use of false identities. Mr. Stanton had always provided as many credit cards, driver's licenses, etc. prior to the start of an assignment as Jack thought he might need. Money was no object. Nor should it be, Jack thought, given how much The Organization was charging clients for their services.

For this assignment, Jack's plan was to use one identity to fly to Pittsburgh, and then a second to complete the trip to Vegas. Upon (hopefully) successful completion of the job, Jack would use the same method to return: two entirely separate identities and a different intermediate city, then a flight into Logan to be followed by the drive north to New Hampshire.

Jack used one of his disposable credit cards to purchase the ticket for the first leg of his trip, and then he powered down his computer and tossed a change of clothes and some personal items into a carry-on bag.

After agreeing to work for The Organization, it had taken him a long time to get comfortable with the idea of planning felonies on his personal laptop. But, as with all areas of its operation, The Organization spared no expense to protect its operatives—and itself—from unnecessary risk. Jack was provided a unique and highly secure Internet service that bounced off servers on four different continents, the signal scrambled and then re-scrambled, rendering the electronic footprint anonymous.

Additionally, a cloaking device, so top secret it was supposed to be available only to select NSA and CIA operatives, had been stolen or purchased or otherwise acquired by The Organization. It shielded the information on Jack's hard drive from even the most skilled forensic computer analysis, and once a day eliminated all traces of his electronic activity from the laptop.

Everything.

After a career spent working in the ultimate risky business, Jack Sheridan knew he was as safe with his current employer as it was possible to be. He knew also that The Organization didn't provide their people with such support because they gave a damn about their welfare. It was strictly a matter of self-preservation, so if Jack eventually screwed up and was caught or killed under suspicious circumstances, his link to The Organization would be untraceable and forever hidden.

Jack knew all this; he just didn't care. He was a businessman, after all, and understood the unspoken agreement implicit in relations between an independent contractor and his employer. Each side must bring an item of value to the table, and when that stopped being the case, the arrangement would end. The ultimate symbiotic relationship.

Now ready, Jack picked up the carry-on and walked to his truck. He figured he had just enough time to make one quick stop before heading to Logan and boarding his flight to Pittsburgh.

* * *

When he hired on with The Organization so long ago, Jack had felt that his wandering days were over. He would have to travel for work, of course, but in between jobs he wanted some stability. He wanted to put down roots for the first time in his life since childhood, so he bought a tiny ranch house in a tiny town in southern New Hampshire that was close enough to Boston via Interstate 93 to make meeting with Mr. Stanton convenient, but isolated enough to provide Jack with the solitude he craved when not working.

And that arrangement had satisfied him until very recently. Lately, though, Jack had begun feeling his age. Thirty-six was considered young in most occupations, but the skills critical to the success of a hired assassin—reflexes and stamina, among others—tended to be most abundant in youth, and lately Jack had begun to feel less like a thirty-something than a sixty-something.

He was starting to feel the first nagging sensations of doubt in his own ability, the first inklings that perhaps it was time to close up shop and begin looking for another career. Maybe it was time to think in terms of life span and quality of life.

He was lonely.

Jack Sheridan had been recruited into the highly secretive military organization that had served as the springboard to his current career shortly after his eighteenth birthday. In the nearly two decades since, secrecy and isolation had formed the overarching principles of his life. There had been relationships, but all had been short-lived, and all doomed to failure, as Jack was forced to guard his privacy zealously.

And there was another factor to consider. What kind of man could subject any woman he cared about to the danger and the constant, unrelenting stress of the life of a professional killer?

So the few romantic relationships he had tried to cultivate over the years had fallen apart quickly, leaving him with a sense of loneliness and bitterness that had only grown with each failure. He guessed he couldn't hope to find a soul mate until he had effected a career change. Even then, maybe it was too late.

Jack chewed on these issues as he climbed into his truck and drove downtown. He had intentionally purchased a seat on a late-morning departure out of Logan so that he would have time to stop for breakfast at his favorite restaurant, the Three Squares Diner.

The food at the Three Squares was mouth-watering, the atmosphere warm and inviting, and the diner was located conveniently close to Jack's home. But none of those factors explained why he was such a devoted customer.

He loved the Three Squares for one reason: its owner, Edie Tolliver. Edie had owned the Squares for as long as Jack had lived here, and he found the longtime owner/cook/waitress enchanting. She was strong and independent, friendly and beautiful. She carried a few scars from her past—who didn't by the time they reached their mid-thirties?—but those imperfections only served to make her more attractive to him, not less.

Jack walked through the front door and smiled as Edie spotted him immediately from behind the cash register and sent an enthusiastic wave his way. He guessed she was a few years younger, maybe early thirties. She was petite, with blonde, shoulder-length hair and a shapely body that suggested long hours working out at the gym, although Jack knew Edie spent virtually all of her spare time at home with her young daughter.

There was no Mr. Tolliver. Edie's husband had run off with one of the diner's previous waitresses years ago, shortly after Jack's arrival in town. "And good riddance to him," was all she would ever commit to on the subject. Her husband had left the little restaurant on the verge of bankruptcy, but over time, Edie brought it back from the brink through hard work and sheer force of will.

Edie Tolliver was beautiful and friendly, but Jack had no doubt she could be as tough as nails when she needed to be. She had what the old-timers called "pluck." Jack was fascinated by her.

She finished ringing up her customer and then stepped out from behind the register to seat Jack. He knew there was a hostess somewhere in the place, but even if she had seen Jack enter, she wouldn't have bothered to come over. Edie always insisted on serving Jack herself.

"So, Mr. Big Shot Businessman, how long are you going to be in town this time before you go running off again?" All she knew about Jack was that he was some sort of "corporate fixer," which was as much as he was comfortable letting anyone know. And the job title was reasonably accurate, all things considered.

She led him through the diner and as he followed he took full advantage of the opportunity to watch her walk. It was mesmerizing. "I'm actually on my way out of town even as we speak," he said.

They reached an empty table and she turned to face him. She moved with such quickness and grace he didn't have time to lift his gaze from her butt without her noticing. She grinned wickedly but said nothing.

For a second.

Then she handed him a menu and said, "Let me know if you see anything you like."

She winked and walked away and Jack shook his head, embarrassed and pleased at the same time. He slid into the booth and a moment later Edie was back, carrying a steaming cup of coffee. "Since you're as predictable as the sunrise, and I assume you're in a hurry if you're on your way to an appointment, I took the liberty of putting in your order for you."

Jack accepted the coffee gratefully and returned the menu. "Oh, really? What am I having today?"

"The usual: a three-egg ham and cheese omelet, side of home fries, white toast and coffee."

Jack nodded and Edie said, "Well? How did I do?"

"Perfect, as usual."

Edie grinned and said, "Be sure to let me know if I can do anything else for you." Then she walked away, leaving Jack with wide eyes and his mouth hanging open.

He wasn't so surprised he didn't watch her walk away, though. He just couldn't help himself.

He was half-expecting it when she whirled and winked at him again. Then she disappeared into the kitchen and Jack dug into his food.

9

Twelve miles south of Las Vegas, in the dusty suburb of Overton, Nevada, Victoria Welling was preparing for work while her over-matched window-mounted air conditioner fought a losing battle against the blast-furnace Nevada heat. A piano player at a small lounge on the outskirts of Vegas called Tequila Mockingbird, Victoria knew she had to be on the road within twenty minutes or risk being late. And her manager—a pasty-faced kid named Paul, who looked as though he should be roaming the halls of a local junior high rather than running a tavern—hated tardiness more than just about anything else.

Victoria stepped out of the shower and wrapped a threadbare Elton John towel around her body. The towel had been a gift from her parents more than six years earlier, as she was leaving home in Reading, Pennsylvania to attend the prestigious Juilliard School of Music in Manhattan.

In the beginning, playing piano had been a chore. She was strong-armed into taking lessons at the age of eight by her mother, who believed firmly in exposing children to the benefits of music. Despite her initial reluctance, Victoria quickly became spellbound by the world of beauty her instructor was able to create out of thin air using only her fingers on a keyboard.

She was hooked.

Victoria practiced every day on her own, without being told, and soon her instructor was telling Victoria's mother that she had a real, live prodigy on her hands. Victoria had no idea what that meant, of course; all the eight year old girl knew was that she intended to devote her life to music.

And that was exactly what she had done.

She finished drying off with her Elton John towel, the ratty piece of cloth so old it did little more than push the moisture around Victoria's body. She knew she should have thrown the thing in the trash years ago, and in fact had rarely used it upon her arrival in New York. The idea of Elton John's face being pressed into her naked body had seemed more than a little weird at the time.

But after the accident that had taken the lives of both her parents, that same towel had instantly transformed into one of Victoria's most prized possessions. It was the last gift her mom had ever given her, and one she was determined to keep as long as she possibly could.

She dropped the towel to the floor, feeling her eyes fill with tears as they nearly always did when thinking of her parents. *Why the heck do you torture yourself like this? Just get rid of the damned towel; Mom and Dad wouldn't care!*

The thought had barely flashed through her mind when she knew she would do no such thing. Ever. At least not until the day the cheap cotton simply disintegrated in her hands and fell to the floor as a bunch of thread.

Victoria shook her head, angry with herself at her emotional fragility even now, years after the accident. She dried her lustrous riot of red hair, the ringlets of curls cascading over her shoulders almost as if by magic as she shook her head. Then she slipped into her work uniform: a traditional black-and-white tuxedo. She hated the thing, was certain it made her look like the world's tallest, skinniest, reddest-headed penguin, but there was no alternative, short of quitting her job and moving on.

She liked it here. She didn't want to leave. But Victoria knew the day was coming when she would have to do exactly that.

And soon.

Because yesterday, driving home from the grocery store, she caught a glimpse of her worst nightmare on the outskirts of the city. She had done a double take at the sight of the man walking along the edge of the road, unable to believe her eyes at first glance.

She looked again, more closely, and then a third time as she drove past, willing herself to see someone else.

But it wasn't someone else.

It was him. Joel Stark. He had found her again.

This day was inevitable, one she had known for months was coming, and she had convinced herself she was ready for when it arrived.

She had been wrong.

A shudder ran through Victoria's body, shaking her tall, slim frame from head to toe as she pictured *him,* on the prowl again, lurking somewhere in the desert like a coiled rattlesnake. He was ready to strike, ready to flush her out of hiding once again.

She took a deep breath. Tried to settle her stomach. Failed.

Get a grip, she thought. *You can deal with this. You have to.*

She considered calling in sick and staying home tonight. But what was the point? Stark had somehow tracked her down again, which meant she was no safer inside her apartment than she would be at Tequila Mockingbird.

In fact, the opposite was probably true. At work she would be surrounded by plenty of other people, including the Mockingbird's bouncers, from the moment she walked through the front door until closing time. It would be difficult, if not impossible, for Stark to do what she knew he was in Vegas to do.

Of course, at the end of her shift she would have to get in her car and drive home.

Alone.

In the dark.

Stop it, she thought sharply as she moved through the apartment switching on every lamp. She would flood the interior of the place with a blaze of soothing light so that by the time she came home, in the two-thirty a.m. darkness, she would—hopefully—be able to muster the nerve to enter.

Finally satisfied, the terrified piano player stepped through her door and into the hallway. Pulled it closed behind her. Double-checked the lock and then walked to the building's entryway, where she stared out into the sun-drenched parking lot. The intense afternoon heat had turned the scene into a shimmering, almost hypnotic tableau.

The lot was empty.

There wasn't a soul in sight.

She double-checked. Still nothing. Her stomach rolled like a ship in a storm.

Victoria Welling took a deep, shaky breath and steeled her nerves, then rushed out the door to her car.

10

Blake Arthur Standiford III stood in front of Big Tony Mercadante's desk, hoping like hell he didn't look as nervous and uncomfortable as he felt. He was smarter than the fat prick sitting smugly behind the massive, highly polished piece of furniture, there was no doubt in his mind about that, but Big Tony held all the cards in this particular poker game.

Blake waited silently for Tony to speak, thankful he had elected to wear an undershirt today beneath the custom fitted Izod dress shirt complementing his two-thousand-dollar suit. He was sweating like a pig. He doubted Big Tony had learned about Kathy Saldana's murder—yet—because he had been paying careful attention to the TV news since realizing how badly he had fucked up and had seen nothing unusual.

But with Tony Mercadante, you could never be too sure.

"So," Big Tony began, lacing his meaty hands behind his head and leaning back. He propped his feet up on his desk and the overmatched office chair creaked like it was being tortured. Blake tried to suppress a grin and wondered whether he would be held accountable should Tony impale his fat ass on the metal frame when the chair inevitably collapsed. It would almost be worth it to see the fat fuck suffer.

He waited for Tony to continue and when it became clear the boss was expecting some kind of response, Blake cleared his throat and agreed, "So…" letting the word hang in the air.

Tony's eyes narrowed, glittering coldly, and Blake immediately regretted fucking with him. The boss said, "What's the deal with the Saldana broad? I been getting…reports…about you and her."

"Reports?" Blake wouldn't have thought it possible, but his sweating intensified.

"Yeah. Reports."

"Uh, what kind of reports, boss?"

"The kind that say the two have you have been playing kissy-face around Vegas after I specifically told you to cut her loose. Are those reports true?"

Blake opened his mouth to answer and Tony cut him off with a gesture, like he was karate-chopping a fly. "I wasn't finished talking. I gotta tell ya, I don't appreciate having to repeat myself. Maybe I'm mistaken. Maybe I never said nothin' to you about dropping Shotgun Sammy's skank wife. Lemme check my notes."

Big Tony swung his thick legs off the desk and sat up straight. His feet and his chair legs struck the floor simultaneously, and the resulting sound was eerily similar to that of a gunshot. His eyes never left Blake's.

Despite his best efforts at staying calm, Blake jumped in surprise. Undoubtedly the maneuver was designed to establish Tony's dominance and ensure he had Blake's undivided attention, and Blake had to admit it was effective. He could smell body odor and wondered whether his t-shirt had soaked through yet. Soon rings of sweat would begin to appear under his arms and his dress shirt would never be the same.

Tony held Blake's gaze for another second. Then he glanced down at the empty surface of his desk and said, "Yeah, that's just what I thought. According to my copious notes here, I ain't mistaken. You *have* been seen around town with Shotgun Sammy's skank wife."

The office went deadly silent, the atmosphere heavy and threatening. Tony let the moment drag out and then said, "I told you to quit that bitch. Why haven't you done what I asked?"

"Oh, I have," Blake answered smoothly, knowing he needed right now to give the performance of his life. Big Fat Tony obviously didn't know about Kathy being dead—yet—but he *did* know about Blake still seeing her, and in the eyes of the boss, being disobeyed was almost as bad as killing an innocent person. It could easily lead to *Blake* ending up face down in a hole if he didn't handle the situation properly.

He straightened his tie and squared his shoulders.

Looked his boss in the eye.

And lied his ass off.

"I don't know where you got your information, but I sent her packing just like you told me to. I did it the day after we talked about it. She was, you know, like twenty years older than me, anyway." He put just the right mixture of respect for Tony and scorn for the jettisoned Kathy Saldana into his voice, certain he was knocking this acting job out of the ballpark.

He could handle this fat old rube. He had been banging Kathy Saldana a hell of a lot longer than Big Tony or anyone else in the family knew. He had fooled everyone for months; there was no reason to believe he couldn't sell this ruse just as well.

Tony stared evenly at Blake, a small emotionless grin tugging at his lips. "So you ain't hookin' up with her no more. I just got bad information. That what you're telling me?"

Blake shrugged. "Guess so. I haven't seen her in a while. I assume she's back in LA."

"Back in LA."

"Yep."

"Good, good, glad to hear it." Big Tony gave Blake a full smile now, but his eyes never got the message. They remained flinty and hard as he stared Blake down.

Despite Blake's confidence and the conviction he was twice as smart as his boss, he found himself swallowing nervously.

Big Tony played the moment like a musical instrument, stretching it out for maximum effect. As a master of intimidation himself, Blake could appreciate his boss's effort, although he wasn't thrilled about being on the receiving end.

At last Tony grimaced and said, "You stay out of trouble now. Keep your dick clean, you hear me?"

Blake nodded enthusiastically. The interview was over and he couldn't wait to get the hell out of here. He was almost certain Tony wasn't going to put a bullet in his back when he reached for the door handle, but he didn't want to hang around and give the fat bastard the chance to change his mind. Or to ask any more questions.

"Good," Big Tony said. "Now get the fuck outta here, I got work to do."

* * *

The door thunked closed behind The Stupid Horny Bastard and Big Tony Mercadante took a deep cleansing breath and counted to ten, just like his wife had taught him to do when he was starting to feel like he wanted to shoot somebody right in the middle of the fucking forehead.

That feeling was the stress talking, according to Maria, and if Tony didn't find a way to deal with it, the stress would eventually strike him down with a heart attack, just as it had struck down her father years ago. Of course, Tony had helped the stress do its job with an "accidental" overdose of the old man's prescription heart medication, but Maria didn't need to know that.

After he finished counting to ten, Tony blew out a frustrated breath. *As relaxation techniques go,* he thought, *this one sucks hard.* "That is one arrogant motherfucker," he mumbled under his breath.

He thought about The Stupid Horny Bastard standing not six feet away, lying his ass off, and felt his blood pressure begin to spike again. *He practically invites me to catch him, waving Sammy's skank around like a goddamn American flag, and then stands there like some choirboy and thinks he's conning me with his bullshit song-and-dance routine.*

Big Tony took another cleansing breath and counted to twenty this time. He wanted so badly to stick a gun in Blake Arthur Standiford III's ear that he could hardly stand it.

But farming the job out was the right move.

He hoped.

In any event, he had committed to it, had paid for it, and all he had to do now was wait for the hired gun to come in and take care of business.

But it sure did feel nice, daydreaming about blowing The Stupid Horny Bastard's brains all over his office wall.

11

Buckled into her car and safely on her way to work, Victoria felt the tension begin to melt away. Slightly. She had long ago given up on ever being able to really relax—and that was especially true now that she had spotted Joel Stark prowling the streets of Vegas—but at least inside her car she felt some small sense of protection with the steel surrounding her and the locks engaged.

She pulled out of the Royal Flush Apartments parking lot—in her very rare moments of whimsy, she liked to think of the shabbily constructed development as the *Toilet Flush Apartments*, but that sense of whimsy was notably absent today—and turned toward Las Vegas and Tequila Mockingbird.

Seeing Joel Stark yesterday had drawn her thoughts to her parents, as seeing Joel Stark always did. The two most traumatic events of her life had occurred within weeks of each other back in 2008, shortly after her move to Manhattan to attend Juilliard, and would always be inextricably linked in her mind.

It was late September of her freshman year, and Victoria was having a hard time adjusting to the frenetic pace of life in New York after growing up an only child in a sleepy Pennsylvania town. She phoned home one night, depressed and homesick, and her parents had decided on the spur of the moment to collect Victoria's grandmother and hit the road, traveling to New York to surprise their only child in an attempt to raise her spirits.

They never made it. Driving north on Interstate 95 on a sunny September morning, a tractor-trailer fully loaded with auto parts had lost control for reasons that were never determined. The truck jackknifed, crashing down onto the Welling's car in the adjacent travel lane, killing everyone inside instantly.

Victoria learned of the accident from a grim-faced New York State Trooper. The officer, not much older than she, removed his hat respectfully as he relayed the news that he was very sorry, but Victoria Welling's entire family had been wiped out.

Her eyes filled with tears and she clamped her jaw tightly shut. She would not break down out here in the Nevada desert over a tragedy that was more than half a decade in the past. There was no changing history, no matter how much she might want to.

No matter how much she was to blame.

She made the left and right turns that would take her to Tequila Mockingbird, driving on autopilot as her mind chewed on the ghosts of her past. After burying the rest of her family, Victoria had returned to Juilliard, not because she particularly wanted to, but because she had no idea what else to do.

A family friend in Pennsylvania offered to keep an eye on the Welling house and perform routine maintenance while Victoria was away, and that was fine with her. There was no way she could ever bring herself to live in it again.

Once back at Juilliard, she tried to resume some semblance of a normal life, knowing it would never really be possible. Her anchor had been taken away.

Just a few short weeks later had come the second life-changing event. Victoria was lying on the couch in the ground-floor apartment she shared with three other Juilliard girls. It was a Friday night. Her roommates, by now all close friends, had been trying to keep Victoria busy, knowing how alone she felt and how desperately she missed her family.

The plan for the evening was to attend a concert in Manhattan. The girls had bought tickets for the show right after the beginning of the school year and had been looking forward to it for weeks. At the last minute, Victoria decided not to go. She was exhausted, she said, and wanted to catch up on some much-needed sleep.

Unable to convince her to change her mind, Victoria's roommates had reluctantly left her alone. The moment her friends walked out the door, she changed into a nightshirt and plopped down in front of the TV in the apartment's small living room. An hour later, she realized she had been flipping mindlessly through the channels and could not remember a single detail about anything she had watched.

It was a clear sign of depression, something that had dogged her since coming to New York and had only deepened following her parents' death. She turned off the television, then picked up a book and walked into her bedroom.

* * *

Victoria learned later, through law enforcement and the prosecuting attorneys over the course of two separate criminal trials, the minute-by-minute chronology of the rest of the evening. Her firsthand memory of the events was ugly enough, but she had committed to learning every last detail, not because she *wanted* to relive that night but because she could not stop herself from doing so.

Stark had loitered for hours in an alley across the street from the apartment building. He was twenty-three years old and unemployed, a street punk bouncing from petty crime to petty crime, and he had been stalking Victoria almost from the moment of her arrival in New York. Where he had first taken notice of her was unclear, but he zeroed in on the tall, pretty redhead like a dog chasing a bone.

By the night of the October concert, Stark had been well familiar with all of the residents in the apartment. He took immediate notice of the fact that all the girls had gone out *except* the object of his attention.

He knew she was home.

And she was alone.

Stark waited two hours, pacing back and forth alone in the alley, collar pulled up against the biting fall breeze. By nine p.m. he had had enough of waiting. He stole across the street, unobserved by witnesses.

He disappeared into the apartment's empty courtyard and

headed straight for the redhead's bedroom window. He knew it was her window, because he had watched her through it plenty of times, staring almost as if in a trance as she changed for bed.

Tonight it had been left open an inch or so for fresh air. A locked screen stood between Stark and the object of his desire, but that presented little challenge to an experienced B&E'er. He pulled a switchblade from his jacket pocket and in seconds had removed the screen, cutting it away around the outside of its aluminum frame. Then he pushed up the open window and hoisted himself quietly into Victoria Welling's bedroom.

She felt herself breathing raggedly, choked by the memories of that awful night but unable to stop herself from reliving them. She approached a red light and realized she had nearly arrived at work, with absolutely no memory of the trip. She took a shaky breath and continued toward Tequila Mockingbird as the mental movie of that long-ago night in New York continued to run inside her head.

Victoria had long since dropped off to sleep, her open book tossed onto the bed next to her. She was lying on her side facing the wall and her short nightshirt had ridden up her legs, exposing her pale green panties.

How long Joel Stark had stood inside her bedroom watching her sleep, Victoria was never able to learn. He was waiting for his eyes to adjust to the gloom, or he was afraid of awakening his prey. It might have been as little as thirty seconds or as long as fifteen minutes. To the prosecutors, it was a minor detail, only worth nailing down as corroboration of their timeline.

But to Victoria that indeterminate length of time was just as much a violation as the actual rape. Even now, six years and thousands of miles later, the idea of Joel Stark standing in her bedroom running his eyes across her body like ants over a picnic lunch made her feel sick to her stomach, made her break out in a cold sweat and descend to near-panic.

Eventually, Victoria had rolled over, perhaps sensing something amiss in her bedroom. Who could say? She opened her eyes and gasped at the shadowy figure standing a few feet away, and then that shadowy figure sprang forward.

More than an hour later, when her attacker finally left the

apartment, Victoria staggered to the phone and called 911. By the time her roommates arrived home after midnight, she was sitting at the kitchen table going over the details of the home invasion/rape with a female NYPD detective.

The rest of the night was a blur: cops taking notes, a trip to the hospital, more cops with more notes, and finally, eventually, against all odds, somehow getting back to sleep—when she had believed she might never sleep again—after the sun had come up the following morning.

Victoria hugged herself tightly as she drove, shaking and sweating, determined not to fall apart just before getting to work.

She failed.

*   *   *

After the fall of 2008 and the two events that changed her life forever, playing the piano became more than just a passion for Victoria Welling. It consumed her, offering the rare opportunity to escape the morass of fear, self-pity and self-recrimination she had fallen into.

She was capable of playing virtually any style of music, but her personal favorite was jazz. She loved the distinctive beat and lived for the opportunity to transport her audience through the music, to make them not just hear it but feel it as she felt it, deep in her soul. To *experience* the music.

This was why she loved Tequila Mockingbird. The place was located off the beaten path of the Vegas Strip and represented the antithesis of the glitzy, style-over-substance clubs catering to the tourist trade all over the city. The Mockingbird's clientele was overwhelmingly local, mostly loyal regulars, and Victoria had been given free rein by the club's management to play any music she wished, as long as it kept the customers coming back.

And come back they did. The Mockingbird was almost always packed when Victoria Welling was at the piano, and the long hours she spent sweating at the keyboard in the crowded club were among the happiest of her life.

But not tonight. Tonight, she wasn't feeling the music. Playing was a chore made even more difficult by the near-breakdown she had suffered driving here. Seeing Stark on the streets of Vegas had shaken her badly, despite knowing for months that this day was coming.

It was always coming.

Victoria had enjoyed almost a year of peace and near-normalcy since the last time he found her, during which she had been living and working in Muncie, Indiana. She had picked up stakes immediately—again—and made another random move, this time ending up in the Las Vegas area.

Stark had chased her around the country over the past five years, somehow always managing to find her and flush her out of hiding. After the break-in and rape in Manhattan, he had been apprehended within a week, busted by an NYPD officer while trying to gain access to another young college student's apartment through *her* bedroom window.

Victoria ID'd the man in a police lineup as her attacker with absolutely no uncertainty, and the D.A. had predicted a slam-dunk conviction. "A positive ID by the victim, plus a positive DNA match from semen left on the bedcovers and in Victoria's body, adds up to a sure win," the confident prosecutor had said.

Except it didn't work out that way.

She dragged her thoughts back to the present and played on. The Mockingbird was crowded, as usual, and Victoria felt fairly confident Stark wouldn't dare come in here, even if he had already discovered where she was working. There were too many potential witnesses for him to attack head-on. He preferred darkness for the commission of his evil, where he could slither around like the reptile he was.

Still, the nervousness threatened to overwhelm her. She worked on autopilot, launching into a Scott Joplin medley that never failed to bring down the house. Every time the front door opened she glanced over, praying that she would not—but fearful that she would—see the pitted, scarred face of her worst nightmare.

12

Jack Sheridan strolled through the terminal at Las Vegas's McCarran International Airport, carry-on bag slung over his shoulder. He had spent a good portion of his time in the air sleeping. Dreaming about Edie Tolliver and her adorable little girl and how much he would love to settle down.

Now that he was in Vegas, though, it was time to focus on the job: eliminating a mob guy in a hit the man's own gangland family wanted nothing to do with. Jack had already come up with a couple of potential scenarios by which he could fulfill his assignment, but at this point, things were necessarily fluid. He needed a little "boots on the ground" time before committing to any specific plan.

He dodged fellow travelers and shook his head at the sight of tourists so anxious to begin donating their money to the local economy that they were bellied up to slot machines located right in the terminal building. Jack had never been much of a gambler; he supposed risking life and limb to earn a living by eliminating some of the most dangerous men—and occasionally, women—in the United States might have something to do with that. Adrenaline was easy enough to come by without going looking for more.

As he wound his way toward the exit, he stopped at a newsstand and purchased a small pair of scissors. He ducked into a men's bathroom and locked himself in a stall, then cut up and flushed the ID's he had used to purchase tickets for this leg of the trip.

Then he pulled out a fresh driver's license and credit card—he would be Harry Carson for the remainder of his stay unless he decided to change identities again—and placed them in his wallet.

The entire quick-change operation took less than three minutes, and then Jack was on his way. He rented a car and drove to the Tumbling Dice Motel, located on the outskirts of Las Vegas's southwest side. He had used the motel before when in Vegas on business and liked it. Each unit was a separate small cottage, affording as much privacy as possible under the circumstances.

Once in his room Jack unpacked, an operation that took less than a minute. Then he stepped into the shower to wash some of the miles off his back. He contemplated trying to sleep and dismissed the thought immediately. It was too early and he had slept too much on the way here.

Instead, he elected to get dressed again and go out for a bite to eat and maybe a drink or two. He needed to contemplate his next move and hated sleeping on an empty stomach. Despite not having been to Nevada in years, Jack had spent enough time in Vegas to become moderately familiar with the area; at least that portion of the city outside The Strip, which was constantly evolving.

And Jack had no intention of spending any time on The Strip unless his work took him there. What he had in mind for tonight was someplace more sedate, the kind of place the locals would go to eat and drink and avoid the constant crush of tourism. The locals would know where to go for the best food.

He stopped at the office on the way out to get the desk clerk's opinion on local taverns. The clerk, an older lady with blue-tinted hair who, judging by the tight jeans and t-shirt she was wearing seemed to think she was still seventeen, smiled wryly at his question.

"A place *away* from the limelight?" she said. "Most people who come here want to head straight for the bright lights and the action."

Jack returned her smile. "Not me. I just want a decent meal and a quiet drink. I've got a business meeting tomorrow, and my boss'd flip out if I blew all my per diem at the Sands."

The clerk snapped her gum and chuckled. "You don't get to Vegas much, do ya? The Sands has been gone for years."

Jack shrugged sheepishly, happy to play the ignorant businessman.

"Anyway," the clerk said, "I've got the perfect place for ya. It's called Tequila Mockingbird, and it's just a couple-three miles down the road." She jerked her head in an easterly direction before returning her attention to a stack of paperwork that seemed much too big for a smallish to moderate sized motel like the Tumbling Dice.

He thanked her and turned for the door, and she waved without looking up.

* * *

It turned out the clerk's somewhat vague directions were right on the money, as Tequila Mockingbird was exactly two and a half miles "down the road."

Jack drove into the lot and parked. He liked the place immediately. It had the look of an old-time roadhouse, complete with flickering neon sign at the edge of the parking lot that featured a bird holding a martini glass. Presumably it was supposed to be a mockingbird, but he would have to take that on faith.

The moment he stepped through the door, Jack decided he had been right to trust the blue-haired desk clerk's judgment. The place was the anti-Vegas lounge. No slot machines. No signed photos of celebrities hamming it up with management. No glittering showgirl costumes for the waitresses.

A solid walnut bar, polished to a mirror shine, had been constructed along one wall. The bar ran from the front door all the way to the rear of the room, where it terminated at the entryway to the kitchen. Tables of varying sizes dotted the interior, with a small dance floor almost looking like an afterthought plunked down in the middle of the room.

The wall opposite the bar featured a raised platform with a massive piano placed on top of it. The piano was clearly the focal point of the club and it had been maintained every bit as lovingly as the bar. Seated behind it, her fingers a blur of motion as she ripped through a lively jazz tune, was a slim, beautiful redhead dressed in a traditional tuxedo. Long red curls cascaded over her shoulders, ending a third of the way down her back.

She was stunning.

And she was terrified.

Jack could sense her fear instantly as he met her wandering gaze for a fraction of a second. The music continued, upbeat and catchy, but the eyes of the young woman were haunted pools of blue. They searched the crowd restlessly, stopping on Jack for less than a second before continuing their constant motion.

He stood just inside the door and focused on the beautiful piano player. Her eyes continued to scan and eventually returned to Jack's. She held his stare once again, for the briefest of moments, and then looked away.

* * *

Victoria caught sight of the new arrival the moment he walked in, and why wouldn't she? Her nerves continued to thrum, and despite the fact she didn't expect Stark to show up here, there was always at least the possibility he would. She had learned over the years never to underestimate him; the man might be sick and obsessed but he had proven himself willing to try new things and to approach the object of his obsession from myriad different angles.

So with her nervous system working overtime, she spotted the stranger before he had taken one full step into the crowded club. She locked eyes with him for a fraction of a second and then continued scanning.

A second later, though, she looked back his way. Her eyes were drawn to him although she couldn't have said why. He an average-looking guy: not ugly by any stretch of the imagination, but not strikingly handsome, either, at least not in any conventional sense.

And he was at least ten years older than her twenty-four years. Normally, Victoria wouldn't have given him a second glance. But there was something about him, the way he carried himself; a strength, a self-sufficiency that seemed lacking in most men. When their eyes met, she got the strangest feeling that he could see deep inside her, could sense her pain, could feel her raw emotion.

But then she shrugged off the sensation. She continued playing, entertaining the crowd, her fingers working solely by muscle memory, her guard up, her eyes scanning.

She couldn't afford to lose her focus.

Joel Stark was out there somewhere.

And he was coming for her.

13

Jack had an unobstructed view of the pretty piano player from his corner table. Within thirty seconds of his being seated, a waitress approached, dressed conservatively for Vegas in tight-fitting black jeans and a maroon Western shirt with white embroidery on the breast pocket that indicated her name was Brandy.

Jack grinned at her and said, "Now, that's appropriate. Brandy serving brandy. Your fate was sealed at birth, wasn't it?"

She leaned close and stage-whispered conspiratorially, "Actually, my name's Geraldine, but Brandy fits better on the blouse."

"Ah," Jack answered. "Plus, it's a good conversation starter for a cocktail waitress. Leads to better tips, am I right?"

She laughed. "Hell, yeah. Is it working?"

"That all depends. Steer me toward a good meal and it's working like a charm."

"The Blackjack Burger is always the freshest thing on the menu. It's what the cook likes to eat on his break."

"Blackjack Burger it is, then. And can I get a side of fries and a draft beer with that?"

"You bet."

Brandy turned toward the kitchen and Jack said, "One more thing."

"Yes?"

"The piano player. What's she drinking?"

"Juice is about all I've ever seen her drink." The waitress smiled. "If you're thinking about trying your luck with her, take my advice and save your money. She's not one to mingle with the customers. We've got guys who come in here every night, great-looking single guys who've been trying to get with her and haven't been able to get one foot in the door."

Jack returned her smile. "Thanks for the tip. But I'm not trying to knock down any doors. Just for fun, would you get the young lady at the piano an orange juice?"

* * *

If there was one thing Victoria Welling had mastered—besides playing the piano—it was deflecting the advances of men in bars. The polite brush-off was a talent every woman working as a bartender, cocktail waitress or entertainer needed to master, and after her attack six years ago in New York, learning to let men down easy had become an absolute necessity.

For some reason that remained a mystery to her, she seemed to attract men like moths to a flame. She had no idea why. When she looked in a mirror, she saw a shy girl who was too tall, too redheaded and not busty enough.

She hadn't been with a man since that awful night in October 2008. Hadn't even been out on a date. Just thinking about being touched made her want to gag, made her stomach clench in fear. She would be terrible company for a man.

Plus, running around the country in an effort to stay one step ahead of a madman was her fate. She had long since come to grips with that fact and had accepted that law enforcement could do little or nothing to protect her. Joel Stark was a free man and until he actually did something to hurt her—and by then it would be too late—in the eyes of the law he had every right to go where he wanted, and to do what he wanted.

Given all of that, there was no way in the world Victoria was going to start a relationship with any man. So when Brandy approached the piano carrying what looked like a glass of orange juice on her tray, Victoria's immediate inclination was to tell her to take it back to the bar.

She guessed it had been sent by the stranger with the compelling presence who had entered the Mockingbird a few minutes ago, and when she glanced over to the table where he sat alone, she received confirmation in the form of a friendly smile and a glass raised in acknowledgment.

The waitress set a coaster down on top of the piano and then placed the glass on it. "I told him you wouldn't accept this," she said semi-apologetically. "But he insisted. He said to tell you he doesn't believe in angels, but if he did, he's pretty sure they wouldn't be any more beautiful than the music that comes out of your piano."

Victoria was between songs, and she looked from the glass to Brandy, to the stranger seated across the bar, and then back to Brandy.

"For what it's worth," Brandy said, "you have to give the guy a little credit. It's a better line than what you usually get in a room filled with drunken fools."

Victoria hesitated and looked over at the man again. As when he had entered, she got the strange sensation that he could see inside her. And rather than making her uneasy, that sensation gave her a rare sense of comfort. Of safety.

Surprising herself, she nodded nervously and said, "Sure. I'll take it. I'm kind of thirsty anyway."

Then she surprised herself even more. "I think it's about time for a break," she told Brandy. She took a deep breath and pushed the piano bench back. She stepped down off the platform and walked across the floor to the stranger's table, aware of the look of incredulous disbelief on Brandy's face, as well as the fact that every male regular in the bar was watching her in stunned surprise.

She was as shocked as they were. Seeing Joel Stark yesterday had shaken her to the core, but this was completely out of character.

The stranger stood as she approached and pulled a chair out for her. "I didn't really expect that angel thing to work, but I couldn't come up with a better line on such short notice," he said with a laugh. "And it's true, you do play like an angel."

Victoria returned his smile nervously. "I-I can't sit," she said. "I just wanted to thank you in person for the drink. That was very kind."

"Just a short break? Ten minutes? Surely your boss won't mind a ten-minute break. You know, to rest those fingers."

This time she chuckled. Surprised herself again by sitting. "You've never been to the Mockingbird before." It was a statement, not a question.

"True enough," he said. "You know everyone that comes here?"

She shrugged. "Not everyone, I guess. But I know I would have remembered you." She cast a glance toward the front door and then away. Her eyes had never stopped scanning, even though—or maybe especially because—she was no longer at her piano.

"I never do this," she said apologetically after a short silence.

"Never do what? Take a break? Eat dinner?" The stranger took a big bite of his burger. "Must make it easy to keep off those unwanted extra pounds."

Victoria laughed in spite of herself.

He nodded approvingly. "You should do that more often. Your whole face lights up when you laugh."

Victoria said nothing, the compliment catching her completely by surprise.

"I'm Harry Carson," he said. He gestured at his plate. "I understand you never eat dinner, but I could really use some help with these fries. I had no idea they were going to serve me a metric ton of the things."

She laughed again and reached for a fry. "Yeah, the cook does go overboard sometimes. But I meant I never mingle with the customers. I mean never, ever. And my name is Victoria. It's nice to meet you, Harry."

She offered her hand and he shook it gingerly. "I'd hate to damage those impressive fingers. It'd be just like me to get too enthusiastic and ruin your career. But this truly is my lucky night. I get to enjoy a delicious meal *and* spend it in the company of a beautiful but mysterious piano player."

"Mysterious? I'm not mysterious," she said, scanning the room reflexively. "But I do have to get back to work in a couple of minutes."

"I guess that's not enough time for you to tell me who you're running from." The stranger said it matter-of-factly, as he was popping a french fry into his mouth.

Victoria sat back in her chair, rattled. "Why would you think I'm running from someone?"

The stranger shrugged. Took a drink of his beer. "You're as jumpy as a guy facing a root canal with no Novocain. But, hey, no worries. It's not any of my business anyway, right?"

Victoria chewed on her lower lip, trying to decide whether to take a leap of faith and trust this man she had just met. There was no reason to. None. And yet, he radiated such a sense of strength and calm, she was actually considering it.

"I-I really have to get back to work," she said after a short pause. "Can we talk on my next break?"

The stranger drained his mug. "To tell you the truth," he said, "I really have to get going. I've got to get up early for work in the morning. But I'm starting to develop a real affection for this place. I'll be back tomorrow night if you're going to be here."

"I'll be here," she answered. "And maybe tomorrow you can ask Brandy to add a little vodka to the orange juice."

The stranger laughed and toasted her with his now-empty mug. "A screwdriver it is, then. I'll see you tomorrow night, Victoria. It was wonderful meeting you."

He stood and took her hand one more time, gave it a reassuring light squeeze, and then threw a twenty down on the table and turned toward the door. Victoria watched him go, not wanting him to leave, wondering whether she would still be alive by tomorrow night.

14

Jack hadn't realized how exhausted he was. After leaving Tequila Mockingbird, he drove straight back to the Tumbling Dice, where he planned to spend a couple of hours reviewing his notes on Blake Arthur Standiford III.

Instead he spent fifteen minutes yawning and stretching at the motel room's rickety writing desk before finally admitting defeat and falling into bed. *You're definitely getting too old for this line of work,* he thought.

There was a time, and not that long ago, when he could have flown across the country, worked all night, and then stayed up the entire next day, with little or no effect on his reflexes or deductive reasoning. Both of these were critically important factors for a man in his line of work. Now he could barely keep his eyes open until midnight, and that was after sleeping most of the way across the country on two separate flights.

* * *

Jack awoke refreshed and ready for the day, his concerns about the aging process forgotten, or at least pushed to the side for now.

He stepped into the shower, thinking about last night's odd encounter with Victoria, the beautiful redheaded piano player at Tequila Mockingbird. She was obviously in some kind of serious trouble. Her mannerisms and her nervous scrutiny of the club's interior gave away that fact just as clearly as if she'd climbed to the roof of the club and shouted it to the world.

What kind of trouble the mild-mannered, skittish young woman could possibly be in was a mystery. She was friendly and well spoken, if extremely shy and clearly terrified. The obvious possibility of drugs didn't seem to fit.

Boyfriend problems, most likely. She hadn't been wearing a wedding ring, but it seemed unlikely a woman as stunningly beautiful as Victoria would be alone.

Could that be it? An abusive boyfriend? She had no signs of injury, no obvious cuts or bruises, but Jack had dealt with enough abusers to know that the ones truly dedicated to their sick form of control tended to be extremely cautious, doing their damage in places on the body not easily observed.

Whatever the problem, it seemed clear to Jack that she was in over her head. She had tried to hide her nervousness and fear, but she had done a damned poor job of it and in the process had piqued Jack's curiosity and aroused his natural inclination to protect, to defend, the helpless.

That desire to protect the weak was a strange character trait for a man who made a living by ending human life, but it had been a defining part of his personality for as long as he could remember. The people whose lives Jack Sheridan ended were never innocent, and they were certainly not helpless. In fact, the one thing they all seemed to share was their determination to take advantage of the innocent, to dominate the helpless.

He hated that.

Jack toweled off and began dressing, determined to put the issue of the redheaded piano player to the side, at least for now. As interesting as the issues of girl and her peculiar behavior were, it was important he focus on the task at hand. He was being paid handsomely to accomplish an assignment that had more than a little risk attached to it. If he lost focus, there was every possibility he would never leave Nevada alive.

Jack had already considered a couple of potential scenarios for dealing with a mob killer slated for elimination. As his mind insisted on wandering back to Victoria, the Tequila Mockingbird's beautiful but terrified piano player, he began to wonder if he should consider other, less obvious scenarios. If he could convince her to open up and her problem was what he suspected it was—abusive boyfriend—perhaps there was a way to assist the young woman while at the same time executing his contract...

He shook his head, angry with himself. *Forget about the redhead for now. Focus. You have no idea what she's afraid of, anyway. Maybe she's just a lunatic.*

He didn't think so, though. He didn't think she was crazy at all. She struck him as a frightened young woman who felt she had nowhere to turn.

Jack glanced out the motel room's window to see a beautiful, sunny Southwestern morning. It appeared the weather was going to cooperate. He picked up a light jacket and walked out the door. It was time to find a coffee shop and then get to work.

*   *   *

Blake Standiford sat in his kitchen, sipping his morning coffee and thinking about Kathy Saldana, and what she had forced him to do to her. It was an indication of how much she had meant to him, he felt, that he was wasting any time at all on her memory.

He was a good-looking guy, smooth, successful with the ladies, and when he left a woman behind, he typically didn't spend one single second of his valuable time mooning over her loss. There were too many other chicks to be had. He went through them like most men went through deodorant.

Of course, he had never actually *killed* a former lover before, but he supposed it had only been a matter of time before that was bound to happen. Blake had always had a temper like a lit fuse, and after a while, killing people and getting away with it had become so commonplace that offing a bitch who had done him wrong was probably inevitable.

But to spend time actually reflecting on his relationship with Kathy surprised him. He had expected to worry a little about Fat Tony and his minions—not that he couldn't handle those idiots—but this trip down memory lane regarding Shotgun Sammy's dim-bulb wife was a bit of a shock.

Whatever.

Blake forced the stupid bitch out of his thoughts and turned them to where they belonged—the shitstorm that was going to rain down on him when her body was discovered. He had hung the DO NOT DISTURB sign on her Luxor door when he left, but that was only going to delay the inevitable, and probably not for very much longer.

Blake knew he would be all over the surveillance videos. The Luxor was like any modern hotel, lousy with CCTV cameras, and somewhere there would be video evidence of the hallway in front of Kathy's room. The video would be time-stamped and would show the two of them entering, and then him leaving alone less than an hour later.

He would be the prime suspect.

He would be the only suspect.

That went not just for law enforcement, but for Big Tony's organization and Shotgun Sammy's, too. Within hours of the murder being discovered, Blake would become very popular with all the wrong people.

It would probably happen sometime today. The odds of it taking longer than twenty-four hours for a corpse to be discovered in a place like the Luxor were extremely slim, DO NOT DISTURB sign or no DO NOT DISTURB sign.

Big Tony would then have some very serious questions for him. But he wasn't worried about Big Tony. He had been handling guys like Tony Mercadante his whole life, using either charm or intimidation. Sometimes both. And he had every confidence he could continue to do so now, at least until he could steal as much cash as possible from the fat bastard and disappear forever.

The trick would be to stay out of custody, while simultaneously staying out of the clutches of Shotgun Sammy's men, who were about to descend on Vegas like a fucking plague of locusts.

It wouldn't be easy, but it was doable. And Blake knew he was just the guy who could pull it off.

* * *

After draining his coffee, Jack set off in the direction of Blake Arthur Standiford's home. The packet of information he had received from Mr. Stanton included a recent photo of Standiford as well as the man's address. He lived in North Las Vegas, in his deceased mother's house, and although traffic was heavy, Jack needed to begin getting a handle on the man.

Part of him wanted to simply walk into Standiford's house, catch the man off guard, and put a couple of slugs in his head. It would be quick and easy, and he had no doubt he could pull it off.

The problem was that handling the assignment with such a brutal lack of subtlety would open up all sorts of complications: potential witnesses, potential collateral damage. Potential risk of the sort that was easily avoidable with a little patience and a professional approach.

Jack entered Standiford's neighborhood and slowed his rental. Pulled to the curb and parked just around the corner from the target's house, leaving himself a clear view of the front and side. The neighborhood was busy, blue collar, with lots of traffic at this time of the morning. All the activity served to make Jack as close to anonymous as he was likely to get in the light of day.

Standiford's home was, like virtually every other house in the neighborhood, Spanish-style single-family stucco construction. The houses looked as though they had probably all been built at the same time, likely by the same builder, in a frenzy of activity during one of the many boom periods in Las Vegas's history.

The target's house was set back less than twenty feet from the road, bordered closely on both sides by neighbors' homes. The properties were separated by a thin screen of full-grown shrubs in desperate need of trimming. A concrete driveway, stained from decades of dripping motor oil, led to a one-car attached garage. The front door featured a small covered archway meant to protect the occupant from the weather—or more likely the blazing sun—while searching for his keys.

It would also serve to shield Jack nicely from prying eyes should he choose to use that entrance to access Standiford's home.

Jack settled back in his rental car, waiting for Standiford to put in an appearance. The desert air was warming rapidly, and he pictured Edie Tolliver scraping frost off her windshield in the chill of a New Hampshire early morning as she prepared to drive to the Three Squares Diner. New England born and raised, he had never lived anywhere else except for his years in the military. Didn't think he wanted to, either, but he had to admit he could get used to this weather.

His reverie was cut short when Blake Standiford's garage door rumbled slowly up on its tracks, revealing a silver Mercedes SL55 convertible roadster inside. The car backed hastily out of the garage, moving much faster than Jack would have done. Jack squinted in concentration. The driver was definitely Standiford.

The car slowed for just a moment as Standiford pressed a button on a remote clipped to his windshield visor. The big door began closing. Then the target stomped on the accelerator and the sports car backed into the street and roared away in the direction of downtown, buzzing right past Jack. The driver never saw him, though, as he stared steadfastly through the windshield, glancing neither left nor right.

Jack debated following, but decided to stick with his original plan, which was to familiarize himself with the inside of his target's home. Most accidental deaths occur in the home, making it the obvious first choice. His contract failed to specify any method for its execution, and Jack's default preference was for the appearance of an accident whenever possible.

His reasoning was simple: if the authorities didn't consider the death to be a murder, they wouldn't be looking for a murderer. And while Jack possessed the utmost confidence in his ability—honed over countless military and civilian missions—to escape detection, there was no reason in the world to tempt fate, either.

The information Jack had received from Mr. Stanton indicated that once Standiford left his home in the morning, there was virtually no chance he would return until much later in the day, probably not until evening. Still, Jack waited a few minutes. He wanted to give the early morning rush of commuters a chance to dissipate, as well as allow for the possibility of Standiford forgetting something and returning home.

After twenty minutes, both considerations seemed to have been satisfied. Automobile traffic had slowed to a trickle, and Standiford was still nowhere to be seen. If he had not turned around by now it seemed unlikely he would.

The neighborhood had by now cleared out to the point where it resembled a ghost town, which presented obvious problems. While a large crowd meant many potential witnesses, it also offered the advantage of anonymity. Citizens could be depended upon to mostly mind their own business when surrounded by throngs of people.

On the other hand, in a nearly empty space the stranger to the community tended to stand out; the man loitering with no apparent purpose became instantly memorable. But one thing everyone understood, no matter the surroundings or the situation, was the officious, self-important bureaucrat.

The representative of the state. The enforcer of regulations.

Inevitably, citizens seeing such a man—or woman—would be concerned about only one thing: that the visitor's sudden appearance be meant for someone else. Anyone else. Once it was established that the stranger wasn't here to see *them,* the bureaucrat tended to fade into anonymity again.

Jack had used that knowledge to his advantage many times, and he knew it would be just as effective today. He grabbed a briefcase and the picked up a clipboard off the front seat, to which he had attached a wad of official-looking but meaningless papers. He stepped out of the car and strode purposefully past two houses to Standiford's driveway, where he turned and marched to the front door.

He resisted the urge to look around and see if he was being watched. He was a census taker, or a building inspector, or any one of a dozen paper-pushers who might have occasion to visit a homeowner on a typical weekday morning. As such, it made no difference whether anyone saw him. Believing it meant selling it, and he wanted to appear as though he had every reason in the world to be on Blake Standiford's front doorstep.

Once he was safely under cover of the portico, the odds of being seen—and thus being interfered with—became practically nonexistent, and Jack relaxed. The front door was positioned in such a way that he was now invisible to neighbors, including residents of the house located almost directly across the street.

The only way *anyone* would see him at this point was if they happened to look at Standiford's front door as they were driving or walking past. And even then their eyes would have to penetrate the relative gloom of the shade provided by the portico.

Jack would need only a few seconds to gain entrance. He removed his lock-picking tools from the briefcase and less than a minute later stepped through the door and into Blake Standiford's front hallway. Set the briefcase on the floor and closed and relocked the door. Mr. Stanton's packet of information had included the helpful tidbit that Standiford hadn't ever bothered to install an alarm system, so there wasn't even that relatively minor annoyance to deal with.

It never ceased to amaze Jack that the worst lawbreakers tended to be the most lax when it came to home security. Logic dictated it should be the other way around, but experience had taught him that the criminal element as a general rule tended to be overconfident and not particularly bright.

Dangerous and cunning, maybe. Deadly, occasionally. But usually not particularly bright.

He stood quietly just inside Standiford's front door, getting his bearings while absorbing the cool stillness of the home. He knew his target lived alone and had no steady girlfriend—at least not since he had murdered her—so there was no reason to believe anyone would be here. Still, he tried never to take anything for granted. Surprises were an occupational hazard that could never be ruled out.

He breathed slowly, listening for anything that might indicate the presence of another human being. Running water. Voices. Footsteps.

He stood in his tracks for three solid minutes, getting the feel for what he now knew to be an empty house. Finally satisfied, Jack began moving quietly but methodically from room to room, committing the layout and furnishings to memory.

He took his time and did the job right. It was quite likely that the next time he entered it would be the middle of the night. He slipped on a pair of surgical gloves, opening drawers and examining closets. Jack smiled at the number of weapons Standiford had squirrelled away. The guy was either one paranoid dude or one of the most dedicated handgun aficionados in Vegas.

He found a Walther P22 in the downstairs coat closet and slipped it into his pocket. The gun was a compact .22 caliber pistol weighing just fifteen ounces, and Jack had the vague suspicion it might come in handy at some point. Standiford would almost certainly never notice the gun had disappeared, nor would he likely think anything was amiss if he did. He would assume he had placed it somewhere else among the many backups stashed around the house.

Thirty minutes later Jack had completed his reconnaissance. He exited Standiford's home as he had entered, through the front door. Using the rear entrance would only invite suspicion if anyone happened to see him. He pulled the door closed and then turned and double-checked to be certain it remained locked.

Then he picked up his briefcase and walked briskly away from the house, just an anonymous city official doing an anonymous job. He kept his clipboard with its official-looking but meaningless papers prominently displayed, but quickly came to the conclusion his little act was wasted. There was no one around to see him. The neighborhood was still deserted.

When he reached his rental, he unlocked the doors and tossed his clipboard onto the front passenger seat. He climbed in and started the car, and then drove off initially in the same direction Blake Standiford had gone almost an hour earlier.

But while Standiford had presumably continued into Las Vegas proper, Jack headed back toward the Tumbling Dice Motel. He had some preliminary planning to do.

15

Victoria Welling looked a mess. She knew she looked a mess, although she hadn't quite been able to work up the courage to check her reflection in a mirror yet.

But she wasn't surprised. Looking like hell was the natural result of sleeping a total of maybe three hours overnight. It hadn't been three straight, uninterrupted hours, either. More like twenty minutes here, a half-hour there, her fitful dozing interrupted by a series of hellish nightmares that had caused her to awaken screaming at least three times.

She had been dreaming about *him*. And that was no surprise, as Joel Stark had dominated her thoughts and fears since that heart-stopping moment when she first spotted him. Last night after leaving work, Victoria had been anxious and afraid, on the lookout for her Man of a Thousand Nightmares the entire drive home. By the time she entered the Royal Flush parking lot, her hands had been shaking so badly she could barely control the vehicle.

Then came the real adventure: getting from the relative safety of her car to the relative safety of her apartment. Her legs wobbled, making her feel like she was going to crash to the pavement at any moment, and her stomach rolled exactly as it had done the time she was twelve and rode the Tilt-a-Whirl at the state fair three times in a row. She puked her guts out that day, and Victoria felt last night like she might do exactly that as she hurried across the poorly lit parking lot.

But she made it, and by the time she had entered her apartment Victoria was sweating like she had just run the New York Marathon. She managed to complete a thorough check of the place—easy enough to do, considering it was roughly the size of a broom closet—before falling onto her bed fully clothed and crying herself to her nightmare-plagued half-sleep.

Now, sitting at her kitchen table nursing a cup of green tea and fearing to look in the mirror, Victoria considered for perhaps the millionth time over the last six years how her life had managed to spiral so completely out of control.

The prosecution of her rapist was supposed to be a slam-dunk. Those were the exact words used by both the investigating officer, Detective Bancroft, and the Assistant District Attorney who had prosecuted the case, Ed Melvin. "Slam dunk." Between the positive identification of her attacker and the DNA recovered from her body, there was no question Joel Stark would be convicted and would spend a very long time behind bars.

Slam dunk.

Except that wasn't what happened.

Right from the start of the first trial, everything had gone horribly wrong for the prosecution team, which hadn't realized one critically important fact: Joel Stark had a twin brother. An identical twin brother named Jason Stark. Jason also lived in New York, and he also had no alibi for the night in question.

And there was more. In an Orwellian twist that the prosecutor's office said they had never before encountered, and that caught them completely by surprise, the twin brothers *shared identical DNA.*

The end result was that the slam-dunk, the supposedly open-and-shut airtight case, began unraveling immediately and never stopped. The state could not prove beyond a reasonable doubt that Joel Stark—and not his brother Jason—had committed the crime. The trial ended in a hung jury, resulting in humiliation for the district attorney's office.

Victoria was devastated. She could still recall, even now, years later, the physical feeling of violation that had come roaring back with the trial's result. She could still recall her exact words to prosecutor Ed Melvin: "How is it possible he can just get away with it? Does the DNA thing mean he's invincible? That he can do whatever he wants and as long as his brother's available to provide reasonable doubt he'll escape consequences?"

The state's attorney had looked away, his silence saying more to Victoria than words ever could.

There was a second trial. The state's attorneys hammered hard at Joel Stark, but in the end, the result had been the same. The jury was unable to reach a verdict.

Ed Melvin and company promised Victoria they would not give up, that Joel Stark would commit more crimes and that when he did, they would be waiting to put him away, but that was small comfort for the devastated victim.

After the second trial, the soon-to-be-freed Stark had looked Victoria in the eyes and mouthed, "I'll see you soon," from across the courtroom. At that moment she had known exactly what she had to do. The sociopath made it perfectly clear he would not stop until he possessed her, likely until he raped her again and this time killed her.

The authorities had made it equally clear there was nothing they could really do until he *had* killed her. And Stark would soon be a free man. Just like that, Victoria Welling's time at Juilliard came to a close, as did any semblance of a normal life.

Within a week of the second trial's end, she packed up all her belongings and left New York in her little Pontiac Sunbird, a high school graduation present from her parents, taking off for parts unknown. The decision was an easy one. As close as she had become to her roommates and fellow Juilliard students, their lives were now foreign to her. And there was nothing else holding her in New York.

She meandered down the east coast, eventually winding up in Tallahassee, finding work playing music in a college bar and slowly beginning to rebuild her life. Dating was out of the question, of course, but her time in Florida was good, bringing Victoria some much-needed rest, and even—after a while—a little peace of mind. It never occurred to her in those early days of her nightmare that Stark might actually come after her, that his obsession could be that all-consuming.

She spent almost a year in Tallahassee. Eventually she got to the point where she would occasionally go almost an entire day without thinking about Stark or his attack on her at all. She still didn't date; couldn't stomach the thought of a man touching her, and the concept of trust was one she doubted she could ever relearn, but under the circumstances, Victoria thought looking back on it, she was almost happy.

And that made it all the more horrifying when she glanced up from her piano one night at work and saw *him*. She froze in mid-song that long-ago night in Tallahassee, simply seized up, something she had never done at the keyboard, not even when she was ten years old playing piano recitals in front of a dozen bored parents.

The club was busy that night, crowded, and there had been noise and confusion, and when Victoria saw him her hands had hung suspended over the keys for a moment and then come crashing down on them. She leapt to her feet so violently that she had given herself deep bruises on the tops of both thighs from where she slammed them into the piano.

To this day, Victoria had no idea how he found her, living quietly more than a thousand miles from New York. She was utterly surprised and totally devastated. She left the club in a panic and never returned, not even to pick up her final paycheck.

This time when she hit the road, she did so with the knowledge that she had a pursuer, someone to whom literally nothing mattered other than finding her and doing . . . something . . . to her. Why he was so fixated on her she had no idea, but there was no sense in kidding herself, because kidding herself just might get her killed.

A series of moves followed, random stops in random places for periods of anywhere from three months to eighteen months. Victoria never allowed herself to get comfortable, never allowed her guard to drop. She traveled from Tallahassee to Fort Worth to Muncie, Indiana, to Fargo, North Dakota, to Oakland to Las Vegas.

She sat at in her tiny kitchen and sipped her cold tea and knew it was time to run again. She drained her mug and put her head in her hands and started to cry. She was exhausted from running, tired of being afraid, and heartsick from the knowledge her ordeal could only end one way.

After a while she forced herself out of her chair. Trudged to the sink and rinsed her mug. It slipped from her fingers and clattered onto the stainless steel and she jumped, startled. She had only seen Stark the one time in Vegas—so far—but once was enough. He was somewhere close and he would be coming for her. When he did, she had to be long gone.

The problem was she had no idea where to run next. She wiped her eyes with the back of one hand and turned toward the bathroom. It was time to shower and prepare to face the day. She would give her notice at work tonight, pack her few belongings tomorrow, and then hit the road again.

For somewhere.

16

Blake drove to work via his usual route, which bypassed the Las Vegas Strip entirely. Like most residents, Blake Standiford tended to avoid that particular area like the plague unless he had a specific reason for being there.

Instead, navigating on autopilot while he considered the problems the day might bring, he stuck to neighborhoods most tourists would never see unless they had somehow gotten hopelessly lost. The route took him past the warehouses, power plants, distribution centers and other structures that would hold no interest whatsoever for vacationers.

It was in one of these areas, a few blocks that might as well have been a million miles away from the strip, that Big Tony Mercadante's base of operations was located, and where Blake was currently headed with so much on his mind. He turned into a well-maintained parking lot surrounded by a chain-link fence complete with razor wire encircling the top and a small guardhouse manned by armed security.

The kid at the gate recognized Blake and opened it so quickly Blake almost didn't even have to slow down. Blake offered up a dismissive wave as he passed. The guard had only been with Big Tony's family a few months, thus making him unworthy of even a second's full attention.

Blake nosed the Mercedes into a parking spot outside an enormous cinderblock building. The words *Great Southwest Import-Export Company* were emblazoned in gold on a massive handmade wooden sign hanging over the entrance, a sign Big Tony had commissioned himself and of which Blake thought the fat fuck was overly proud.

Blake climbed out of his car and walked quickly toward the office. He was late, as usual, and while he normally didn't give a damn about being on time, he thought it might not be the best idea to push his luck with Tony, given the Kathy Saldana mess.

He slowed as he walked through the door. The interior of *Great Southwest Import-Export* was a flurry of activity, as always. The company had a hand in dozens of business ventures, some of them even legitimate. The various enterprises made laundering money easy and went a long way toward explaining the presence of armed guards outside what was essentially nothing more than an office building.

Blake had decided the best way to approach what he hoped would be his last day in the employ of Fat Tony Mercadante was to act as though everything was completely normal. If anything had changed as far as Tony learning Kathy Saldana's fate, Blake knew he would find out about it soon enough, and he would deal with the fallout then.

He would shoot his way out of here if necessary.

He didn't think it would come to that, though. The Saldana bitch had been dead long enough that it was simply inconceivable the news had not made its way to Tony yet. Blake was still alive and kicking, which meant the fat bastard believed his story about breaking it off with Kathy. The fact that she had been murdered in Vegas was nothing more than an odd coincidence.

And if Fat Tony harbored any suspicions? Blake would do what he had been doing his whole life and lie, bluff or bluster his way out of trouble. He only needed to string the old asshole along for a day. That would be enough time for Blake to get his shit together and disappear. Maybe go to New York, where some of the outfits still had an appreciation for a man of his talents and abilities.

In the meantime, treating today as just another workday meant checking in at the *Great Southwest* offices to receive his instructions. As one of the higher-level employees who was still not part of the Mercadante family's inner circle, Blake's duties included but were not limited to ferrying drugs, guns, betting slips, cash, sometimes even people. Usually it was a combination of the above.

Often his duties included intimidating or hurting people.

Sometimes they included eliminating people

Obviously the job had the potential to be dangerous, given the illegal nature of most of his assignments and the fact that he was constantly coming in contact with some of the seediest members of Nevada's criminal class. A few of the people he dealt with were even more sociopathic than he, and that was saying something.

But he rarely felt in danger. Big Tony Mercadante was one of the most feared men in the Vegas underworld, and everyone Blake dealt with, from the lowliest scumbag drug dealer to the highest-level casino contact handling the most outrageous sums of money, was well familiar with his employer and what the response would be should Blake Standiford be treated with anything less than the utmost professional respect.

By the time he had entered the building, Blake's hurried walk had turned into a measured strut. He had an image to maintain among the grunt-level guys in the family, and that was exactly what he was going to do.

A receptionist's station was located in the middle of the lobby. Sitting behind the desk, surrounded by telephones, computers and a fax machine was a harmless-looking little man, prematurely balding, who sported the most ridiculous-looking black horn-rimmed glasses Blake had ever seen. He looked like a bad Elvis Costello impersonator.

The man's name was Janousz, and his current position with the Mercadante family was combination receptionist/armed guard. The improbably named little man was tasked with preventing anyone who wasn't supposed to be here from venturing any farther into the building.

Blake hated him. The guy had immigrated to the States from somewhere in Eastern Europe, and as far as Blake was concerned, he should have stayed there. He had no idea what Big Tony saw in the guy. His English was terrible and he looked like he'd struggle to beat up a ten-year-old even if the kid spotted him the first punch.

Blake did, however, very much enjoy fucking with the guy. He took particular pleasure in addressing him as "Janice," although— or maybe because—the dumb foreign fuck never even seemed to realize he should be offended by the term. Now, as he slowed slightly on his way past the reception desk, Blake said, "Yo, what up, Janice?"

The mild mannered-looking fellow blinked behind his comically large glasses and said, "You are to go to Big Tony's office, yes?" With his accent it sounded like he was saying "Beeg Toonee".

Blake stopped and shook his head. Glanced at Janousz scornfully. Scratched his armpit. "So, I am to go to Beeg Toony's office, do not pass go, do not collect two hundred dollars?"

The overmatched foreigner wrinkled his forehead in confusion. "What is 'pass go and collect two hundred dollars'? And the name is Janousz. Janousz." The words came out, "Waaht ees 'pess gou andt collect two hahndredt dollars'? End zee name ees Yah-noosh. Yah-noosh."

Blake smirked. "It's just an expression my friend, don't you worry your pretty little head about it. Nice talkin' to ya again, Janice."

He turned toward the hallway leading to Big Tony's office, mumbling just loudly enough to be sure he was overheard. "Jesus, what a fuckin' dope."

* * *

Janousz Bejko stared through narrowed eyes as the blonde-haired idiot walked away. He understood a lot more English than Blake Standiford realized, certainly enough to know when an arrogant ass was belittling him. He longed to be given the latitude to handle Standiford in his own way, but thus far hadn't risen high enough in the Mercadante family to have earned such a privilege.

It wouldn't take long, though. Despite his meek appearance and slight stature, Janousz Bejko was in reality one of the most accomplished hitters in all of what used to be known as the Communist-bloc countries. He was smart and ruthless, and Big Tony Mercadante had been recruiting him for a position in Vegas for years. Six months ago he had accepted Tony's offer and started a new career—or, more accurately, a new extension of his old career—in the States.

His current position, manning the front desk at *Great Southwest Import/Export* was strictly temporary. Tony had explained it was the best way he could think of to make Janousz comfortable in his new surroundings and also allow him to become familiar with his coworkers.

Janousz understood and appreciated Tony's intentions. But he had had enough of sitting around buzzing people into and out of offices, checking IDs and sending unwelcome visitors on their way. He was ready to begin taking on more interesting jobs, and he was hoping against hope his first assignment might be to take down that miserable little bastard Blake Standiford III.

* * *

Big Tony Mercadante watched Blake through narrowed eyes as the loose cannon entered his office. Just seeing The Stupid Horny Bastard set his blood to boiling. He knew Standiford had absolutely no appreciation for the difficult position he had put Tony in by killing Shotgun Sammy Saldana's wife, and that knowledge pissed him off almost as much as the fact that Blake had killed an innocent woman.

"You wanted to see me, boss?" The words were out of Standiford's mouth before he was even completely through the door. It was obvious he didn't want to give Tony the chance to speak first.

"Figured that one out, did you?" Tony hated the way Blake strutted round like he owned Vegas. Big Tony, who practically *did* own Vegas, never strutted. He was too large to pull it off successfully and besides, he had long ago come to the realization that the truly successful lawbreakers were the ones who stayed invisible, not the ones who promoted themselves like Hollywood celebrities.

Blake ignored Tony's remark. He stopped at a chair placed in front of the desk and waited for an invitation to sit.

Tony let him stand. "Tell me about Kathy Saldana," he said, staring unblinkingly at Blake through eyes narrowed to slits.

"What do you wanna know?" The Stupid Horny Bastard spread his hands like a priest on Sunday morning.

"Come on, asshole, don't fuck with me. I'm not in the mood. Are you really gonna stand there and pretend you don't know your little extracurricular activity ended up dead on the floor in her old man's room at the Luxor?"

Blake raised his hands again, palms out this time in a gesture of conciliation. "Whoa, boss, hang on. Yeah, I heard she got herself killed, but like I told you before, I stopped seeing her before that." Tony watched as The Stupid Horny Bastard rearranged his face into a rough approximation of sincerity. "It's too bad, but shit happens, ya know?"

Tony snorted. He had to give Standiford credit; the guy had balls. Dumb as a stump, but he had balls. He stared into the man's eyes and said nothing, drawing the silence out. When he spoke, his voice was quiet and measured and filled with menace. "Shit most definitely does happen; yes it does. And more shit than you can imagine in that little brain of yours is going to rain down on you if I find out you had something to do with murdering Shotgun Sammy's wife."

By now Blake was shaking his head firmly from side to side. Tony watched with satisfaction as The Stupid Horny Bastard's carefully constructed veneer of insouciance began to crack. "Nah, boss, don't worry about it. I'm tellin' ya, I was nowhere near her when she bit it. I don't know who did her, but it wasn't me. You ask me, she went looking for love in all the wrong places."

"Yeah, I think we can both agree she did that," Tony said quietly.

Blake stood nervously, fiddling with the end of his tie and still trying to master the look of sincerity.

After a few ominous seconds Tony said, "Okay, fine, whatever. Get outta here. Go see Janousz at the front desk. He's got some shit for you to do today."

The clearly relieved Stupid Horny Bastard exited as quickly as he could without breaking into a sprint, hurrying to the door and almost but not quite slamming it behind him.

As he was walking out of the office, Rudy Palermo entered through a side door. Tony asked, "Did you get all that?"

Rudy nodded. "I got it. He's lying his ass off. He whacked her and now he's trying to figure out how the hell he's gonna save his sorry butt. It's really too bad we can't do him ourselves. There's nothing I would enjoy more."

ALLAN LEVERONE

Tony shook his head. "No," he said with finality. "This way's better. We let the hired help take care of it and stay as far away as we can from the fallout."

After a short silence, Rudy nodded, not that it mattered. They both knew whose decision it was to make. "Yeah, I guess," he said. "But are you sure putting the fear of God in him was the right move? What if he runs before the hired help can finish the job?"

Tony chuckled. "He ain't going anywhere, at least not yet. He thinks he's smarter than everybody else. Right now he's congratulating himself on his brilliant acting job. He figures the fact that he's walking outta here alive today and not being dumped in pieces into a dozen shallow graves means we bought his little song and dance. And there's something else."

"What's that?"

"I *had* to lean on him a little. The Saldana broad's murder is gonna be all over the news today. If word of her death got out and I *didn't* sweat him, even a dumbass like Blake would wonder why. And that *would* spook him, maybe even make him nervous enough to run."

Rudy thought about it for a moment and then nodded again, obviously impressed. "Makes sense," he said. "But I'd still like a crack at the arrogant prick."

Tony laughed, the sound a rumble deep inside his massive chest. "Don't worry about him. We stick with the plan. Standiford will be nothing more than a bad memory soon and keeping our hands clean might be the only thing that saves *our* sorry butts."

17

Impulse control had never been Joel Stark's best personality trait. In fact, just the opposite was true. Failure to think through and consider the consequences of his actions had led to endless problems in school—in those days before he had been kicked out of school—and had haunted him on a regular basis ever since.

It was these impulse control issues that led to his problems with Victoria Welling back in New York in 2008. He regretted them deeply, and why wouldn't he? They had led to a lengthy incarceration while awaiting trial—even with his father's connections, bail had been denied—and then the humiliation of not just one but *two* criminal prosecutions, during which his character was trashed and his life dissected. He had been portrayed as a common lowlife perv.

So he sure as hell did have a few regrets. The home invasion and rape of his little princess wasn't one of them, though. The events of that night had brought him endless pleasure in their second-by-second reliving, and Joel knew without a shadow of a doubt he would do it all over again if he could.

He had made up his mind that long-ago night in her apartment to make the redheaded beauty his—permanently—and once he made up his mind about something, there was no changing it.

What he *would* change, however, given the opportunity, was his modus operandi. He should have been more cautious, should have developed a plan that allowed him to satisfy his desires while at the same time providing the best chance for him to escape the consequences of his actions. Once he was confident he had a workable plan, *then* he should have acted.

It was a hard lesson to learn. Endless hours of reflection in jail drove the message home, but then when he got out and finally tracked his princess down in Florida, so many months later, all of the enlightenment he had thought he gained went immediately out the window. He acted impulsively, going straight to her place of employment, and even worse, allowed her to catch sight of him.

And before he knew it, she was gone, forcing him to skulk back to New York with his tail between his legs and resume his search, starting over from scratch.

The same thing had happened several times since, too, each occurrence reinforcing Joel's desire to make the little bitch his own—*and teach her a much-needed lesson*, he thought to himself bitterly—each failure reminding him how much improvement he still needed to make on that pesky impulse-control thing.

But this time would be different. He had promised himself he would move slowly out here in Nevada and do things right for once, and he was determined to keep that promise. To the best of his knowledge, Victoria had no idea he was here, so there was no reason to hurry. No sense of urgency, beyond his own intense desire to possess her.

Joel was proud of himself thus far. He had known the address of her apartment—assuming she hadn't taken off again already, of course—since before leaving Brooklyn and had thus far managed to avoid breaking into it and dragging his girl out by her hair. He knew where she worked and had likewise managed not to barge into the piece of shit little honky-tonk piano bar and frighten her away again.

And it seemed to Joel that her job was the key to everything. The lounge, which catered to redneck Nevada locals, closed at two a.m., and based on his admittedly incomplete surveillance, it seemed as though she pounded the piano keys right up to closing time when she was working.

This meant she would have to drive home in the middle of the night and then make her way across a poorly lit parking lot during a time when virtually everyone else in her apartment complex would be asleep. That fact would greatly influence how he chose to proceed, something he had decided it was nearly time to do.

But there would be no jumping Victoria in the parking lot, no dragging her into his car and taking off. The old Joel would have done exactly that or something similar without a second thought, but not anymore. Regardless of the lateness of the hour or how tired she was, if he slipped up for even half a second and allowed her a scream, the whole thing would come crashing down on him.

Again.

And that was not going to happen.

He was proud of himself for what he had accomplished in just a few days here in the desert, but it was now time to move. Tonight he would put his plan into motion. Tonight he would finally achieve his long-awaited reunion with his princess. They would share a few days together in her apartment, alone and intimate, allowing them to become properly reacquainted, and then he would determine the appropriate next step.

They would either set off together for some as-yet unknown destination, Victoria by his side where she belonged, or, if she insisted on continuing to resist him, she would find herself buried in the Nevada desert, alone and never to be found.

After all, Joel loved his princess, but even love had its limits.

And he was nothing if not flexible.

18

Jack had discovered early in his career that the doing the prep work was, for him at least, the most tiring part of a job. That it was also critical to achieving success went without saying, and the professional in him would not consider skimping.

After checking out Blake Arthur Standiford III's home, he had taken some time to renew acquaintances with an Organization contractor located in the Southwest, a man who had worked with Mr. Stanton for years and who, it was rumored, possessed the contacts and capabilities necessary to acquire anything an Organization member might need, up to and including an M-1 Abrams tank.

Jack didn't need a tank, though. In fact, he didn't need anything as remotely exotic as a tank. Based on his current plans, which were always subject to revision right up to the moment of their execution, he thought it was quite likely he would need nothing more than a single handgun with a fully loaded magazine.

The Organization contractor was located south of Las Vegas, in Boulder City, and Jack spent his time on the road reviewing what he had learned about Blake Standiford and in particular the layout of the mobster's home. As he did so, he found his mind wandering again and again to the beautiful—and terrified—young piano player at Tequila Mockingbird.

The way she had been acting reminded Jack exactly of the Post-Traumatic Stress Disorder he had seen so much of during his time in the military. The jumpiness, the nervousness, the inability to relax, it all fit. Jack guessed that were he able to get to know Victoria better, he would discover she suffered from bouts of depression and had problems sleeping.

PTSD.

The young woman had clearly suffered some kind of serious trauma, and his guess was that it was boyfriend related. The way she was acting last night, scanning the crowd, keeping an eagle eye on the club's front door, told him she was terrified that the boyfriend would come bursting through the door at any moment, and that when he did, she would be the target of his wrath.

And unless he was way off the mark, it wouldn't be the first time. Not even close to the first time. He pondered the mystery as he drove, and before he knew it, he had arrived in Boulder City. He parked at the agreed-upon meeting place—a fast-food joint—and waited for his Organization contact.

It was a short wait. Ninety seconds after his arrival, a non-descript-looking older man in a nondescript-looking older sedan entered the lot and parked next to Jack's rental. It was the same man Jack had worked with in the past in this area.

The man looked exactly the same as he had half a decade ago, and he was just as cautious as he had been back then, too. He had obviously been parked somewhere nearby watching the lot, wanting to be certain Jack had come alone before revealing himself.

Jack didn't blame him. Caution was critical in this line of work. But he wanted to get today's transaction over with, so he wasted no time stepping out of his car and reintroducing himself to the contact. Twenty minutes later he was driving out of the lot, the proud owner of a brand-new Sig Sauer P229. He hoped it would be all the firepower he would need.

19

Today had been one of the longest days of Victoria Welling's life. She had spent most of it immobile at her kitchen table, staring out the tiny window at the sunbaked parking lot and hoping and praying to come up with some kind of plan for dealing with her awful reality that didn't include running once more like a scared rabbit.

Her prayers had not been answered. She found her thoughts drawn to the mysterious stranger last night at Tequila Mockingbird, the slightly older man who projected such an air of strength and dependability she had abandoned her ironclad policy of not mingling with the customers.

Harry, he had said his name was. Victoria had spent no more than fifteen minutes in the man's company, but it occurred to her now that she hadn't felt as safe as she did in that fifteen minutes since before the night in Manhattan when Joel Stark had stolen her innocence.

Harry had told her he would be back tonight, that he would buy her another juice—this time even with alcohol in it; what the heck was she thinking?—and that they could talk some more. She wondered whether he would keep to his word and show up. And whether, even if he did, she would succumb to those feelings of strength he radiated and spill her guts.

She wanted to, more than anything in the world, but what would be the point? There was nothing he could do for her. It didn't matter how strong he seemed or safe he made her feel, Joel

Stark was a genuine sociopath who had stalked her for years. He would be more than prepared to deal with any interference dished out by a traveling businessman.

And what right did she have to put her problems onto some well-meaning stranger, anyway? He would run like hell when he found out about Stark—at least, he would if he had half a brain—or he would try to interfere and in so doing he would make things immeasurably worse.

Eventually she forced herself to stop thinking about the stranger. It was pointless. She pushed herself out of her chair and tried to keep busy dusting, vacuuming and sweeping. There was no need, the apartment was spotless, but it gave her something to do in an attempt to take her restless mind off Stark.

When she realized she was completing the same set of tasks for the second time—or maybe the third; she couldn't exactly remember—while crying her eyes out, Victoria angrily wiped the tears away with the back of her hand and stalked into her bedroom. Maybe she could manage an hour or two of sleep before getting ready for work. She was certainly tired enough after mostly tossing and turning last night.

An hour later she gave up on the idea. She couldn't sleep, and besides, she knew what was waiting for her if she *was* lucky enough to drift off. *Him.* Joel Stark, star of her nightmares.

It just wasn't worth it. Victoria decided she would rather be tired than suffer that fate. After giving up the possibility of sleeping, maybe forever, she arose and padded to the bathroom. Showered and dried off with her threadbare Elton John towel. Dressed in her tux for what would almost certainly be her last night of work at Tequila Mockingbird.

She circled her apartment exactly as she had done yesterday, switching on lights, making sure every bulb was burning. The two-thirty a.m. darkness was all-encompassing even to people not being stalked by a madman. For Victoria, the idea of entering her apartment at that time of night *without* the lights keeping vigil was inconceivable.

When she had completed her routine she stepped through her door and then closed and locked it behind her. Moved to the building's foyer and stopped, breathing heavily. Her heart felt as though it might explode in her chest. The thought of stepping out of her apartment, even now, in the late-afternoon Nevada sun, was terrifying.

She took a deep breath. Blew it out shakily. Examined the parking lot through the window next to the apartment building's entrance. It was still. Silent. Apparently empty.

She looked out the window again and realized she was stalling, postponing the inevitable. Finally she forced herself into the stifling desert air and sprinted to her car.

20

Jack realized with some surprise that he had been doing no more than passing the time over the last few hours. He told himself he was holed up in his room at the Tumbling Dice finalizing his plan of attack tonight against the doomed Blake Standiford, but the reality was that he had been watching the clock and mostly daydreaming, passing the time until he could head out to Tequila Mockingbird.

The contract Standiford's mob "friends" had taken out on him specified nothing more than that the man's death deflect attention away from his ties to Vegas's Mercadante family. This left Jack with plenty of latitude on how to proceed, and while he had initially considered options like manufacturing a car accident or arranging an unfortunate gas leak and blowing up Standiford's house with him in it, he had come to reject all of them.

Simpler was better. When in doubt, it was almost always more beneficial to choose the less complicated of two options.

That was Rule Number One in the world of the professional assassin. It had been drilled into Jack's head from his earliest days in training with the elite super-secret, technically nonexistent unit in which he served for eight years in the United States military, and it was the pillar around which he had built his civilian business as well.

The implications of the "simpler is better" rule here in Nevada were obvious: manufacturing car accidents and blowing up houses were about as far from simple as an assassin could get, and while those methods had their benefits under the right circumstances, making them happen required time that he didn't have as well as scrupulous attention to detail, and inevitably left the potential for plenty of loose ends.

Loose ends were bad.

So in the end Jack had elected to avoid unnecessary complications. And while simpler was better, it also, by definition, required less planning, which explained Jack's current situation: watching the clock while waiting for the time to get late enough to begin the evening's activities, which may or may not include eliminating one very dangerous Las Vegas mobster.

* * *

Tequila Mockingbird was crowded again. Apparently many of the people who actually lived and worked in Las Vegas had long since eliminated the strip as a reasonable destination for entertainment and a great many of them had chosen this particular club instead. Having witnessed the ability of their dazzlingly beautiful piano player firsthand, Jack wasn't surprised.

He could hear the upbeat jazz piano way out in the parking lot, the music drifting out of the club before he even made it to the door. Once inside, he looked immediately at the raised platform and locked eyes with Victoria.

But only for the barest fraction of a second. Then the young woman's eyes continued their ceaseless roving, scanning the crowd restlessly before darting back to the entrance, even as her fingers danced over the keys.

The big room was jumping and the club was crowded, but within seconds of Jack taking a seat—the small table he had used last night was unattended, so he took it again—his waitress hurried to take his order. She materialized out of the crowd, moving with easy agility, and Jack smiled at her when he recognized the young woman who had served him last night.

"Nice to see you again, Brandy," he said as she slapped a cocktail napkin down on the table.

She returned his smile, shaking her head as she did. "Well, if it isn't our very own miracle man! You gotta share your secret."

"What secret is that?" Jack said playfully, although he knew exactly what she was getting at.

"Give it up, mister! Just how in the world did you manage to convince our little Victoria to spend time with you when so many other guys have gone down in flames?"

"Just lucky, I guess."

Brandy shook her head. "I think there's more to it than that. But I gotta admit, it's good to see that sweet little thing finally coming out of her shell, even if it's just a bit."

"I agree, she sure does seem sweet. But what's her deal, Brandy? She's obviously terrified. What's she so afraid of?"

"Ya got me. She blew into town months ago and hasn't opened up to a single soul that I'm aware of. When she got here she was wound up tight as a drum. Over time she seemed to relax a bit, but all of a sudden now she seems as upset as ever. No idea why, though."

Jack gazed thoughtfully across the room at the piano player, then back into Brandy's eyes. "I guess I'll just have to ask her myself. In the meantime, I'll take another one of those burgers I had last night and a beer. Oh, and would you be so kind as to bring our favorite musician a screwdriver, too?"

Brandy blinked in astonishment. Her expression of surprise was so extreme Jack laughed out loud.

"Are you kidding?" she said after a delay. "Vodka? Save your money my misguided friend, she'll never accept a drink with alcohol in it!"

Jack glanced once more at the piano and found Victoria staring back at him, looking straight into his eyes. He gave her a wink before her restless gaze moved on and her lips twitched in a vague approximation of a smile. He said, "Let's just wait and see, shall we?"

A few minutes later Brandy returned with his order. He thanked her and then passed the time waiting for Victoria's break by studying the redhead as she played. Again she seemed nervous and preoccupied. If anything, she struck him as even more tightly wound than she had been last night, and that was something he wouldn't have believed possible.

Twenty minutes later, Victoria pushed her bench away from the piano and wound her way through the big room toward his table, half-empty drink in hand. The raucous crowd seemed to part before her and, as was the case last night, practically every head turned to follow her progress. She didn't seem to notice.

She flashed Jack a nervous smile as she sat. Even distracted and clearly upset, she had the ability to light up the room with her smile.

Jack shook his head and said, "You have these people eating out of your hands. How do you do it?"

She wrinkled her forehead and swished her drink. Picked up a french fry distractedly, popping it into her mouth. "What do you mean?"

"You didn't notice this rowdy bunch making like peasants before the queen? I'm surprised they didn't bow as you walked past!"

Victoria shrugged and shook her head. She seemed genuinely mystified and Jack chuckled. "Anyway," he said, changing the subject, "I seem to recall you were going to tell me a story tonight."

She trained her gaze on Jack. Dark circles surrounded her eyes and she appeared haunted. Exhausted. "What's the point? I've been running for years now and talking about it isn't going to change anything."

Her forearms were resting on the scarred wooden table and Jack reached out, taking one of her small hands gently into both of his larger ones. She stiffened immediately. He kept his grip loose, giving her the option of pulling away, but to his surprise she didn't.

She had lowered her eyes to the table and Jack said nothing until she lifted her head and looked back up at him.

Then he said, "Listen to me, Victoria. It's obvious you're in some kind of serious trouble. Now, I'm not saying there's anything I can do to help you, but any idiot can see you need to talk to someone, if only to unburden yourself of your fear. You look like you're about to have a nervous breakdown. Who better to talk to than an anonymous stranger you'll never have to see again?"

The bright blue eyes filled with tears and after a moment the young woman started talking. She told him about New York.

She told him about Joel Stark.

She told him everything.

* * *

By the time Victoria finished speaking, nearly thirty minutes had elapsed. Jack listened quietly, interrupting only occasionally to ask a question or clarify some point. Mostly, though, he let her purge herself of her demons.

When she had finished the story, Jack stared into her beautiful, haunted eyes. "Are you telling me this slimeball got off because he shares DNA? How is that even possible?"]

Victoria shrugged. She still hadn't removed her hand from Jack's. She seemed to be drawing strength from him, looking more composed already than at any time since Jack had first seen her. "That was my exact question to the prosecutor. Nobody could ever answer it to my satisfaction, certainly nobody in the DA's office."

"And now he's following you around the country? For what purpose?"

"I don't know. I can only assume he wants to finish what he started. To be honest, Harry, I haven't waited to find out. Whenever I see him I move on, like I should have done already this time. But . . . I don't know . . . I like it here in Vegas, and I'm just so tired of running . . ." She shook her head bleakly, the rich red mane of curls framing her pale but pretty face. "I just don't know what to do."

Victoria's break time had long since ended. A man Jack pegged as the club's manager watched them from behind the bar, clearly unhappy his entertainer had stopped entertaining. Jack gave her hand an encouraging squeeze and her face lit up in a brief, trembling smile. Then it was gone.

She took a deep breath and said, "I think I'd better get back to work before I lose my job. I'll be leaving soon enough anyway, but I've never been fired in my life and I'm not going to start now."

Jack gave her hand one final squeeze and then released it. "You go make some musical magic, and for now at least, you can stop worrying. I'm not going anywhere yet and I promise you Joel Stark won't get near you while I'm here."

"Thank you," she said simply. She stood and turned back toward the piano. Jack watched her as she walked. She was still checking the bar for strangers but not, he thought, with the manic intensity she had displayed before. She glanced back once, almost as if to convince herself he was still there, and then sat and began to play.

Jack considered her story in amazement, He had seen and heard a lot in his thirty-six years, but this young woman's story beat them all. In spite of her apparent fragility and obvious fear, Victoria was one tough cookie to have survived as long as she had after being abandoned by the very justice system that was supposed to protect her.

He wondered how she was able to change gears so quickly. She went from pouring her heart out about rape and brutality and injustice to playing a light, bouncy jazz tune that had everyone inside Tequila Mockingbird clapping along and stomping their feet in a matter of seconds.

He couldn't believe the absurdity of her situation, but he had already decided to help her.

Who else would?

21

The crowd had thinned considerably by the two a.m. closing time. There were still a few hardy souls left inside Tequila Mockingbird, but most of the exuberant partiers had gone home. The people left at this time of night were the hard-core drinkers, the ones whose focus mostly seemed to be inside themselves.

Victoria understood that. She spent a lot of time inside herself, too.

There was one notable exception, though. True to his word, her new friend Harry Carson had stuck around all night. He sat quietly at his small table, drinking coffee after finishing his one beer, and watching out for her. He had bought her a second drink an hour or so after she finished the first one, and she had surprised herself again by accepting it.

Now the faintest remnant of the pleasant vodka buzz remained. Her face was flushed slightly from the alcohol, she could feel it, but she didn't care. The drinks hadn't interfered with her work. She was far too talented a musician to be affected in a negative way by two screwdrivers, even though she couldn't remember the last time she had had so much as a sip of alcohol.

What the drinks *had* helped her do, though, was relax and unburden herself to Harry over the course of two more short breaks. She didn't know what to think about the fact that she had spilled her guts to a total stranger, but the fact of the matter was she felt better over the last couple of hours than she had at any time since seeing Joel Stark again.

But now, as she closed the piano cover over the keyboard and stood, Victoria felt the familiar sense of depression and fear begin to rise in the pit of her stomach. Tonight had been wonderful, something she desperately needed, but it was nothing more than a temporary interlude. The reality was simple: Stark was out there somewhere and he was closing in. His history suggested he was not going to track her all the way to Vegas and then just sit around.

He would act soon. Maybe very soon.

So, while Harry was incredibly sweet, drinking his coffee and watching over her, listening patiently to her sob story, the fact of the matter was she was no better off now than she had been before he showed up. He couldn't watch over her forever, and when he walked out of here tonight, she would be just as alone as she had ever been, and in just as much danger.

She trudged across the nearly empty club and flashed Harry a tired, crooked smile. "I can't believe you're still here."

"I told you I would be, didn't I?"

Victoria was amazed. The man didn't appear tired at all. He looked fresh and alert, like he had just arisen from a good night's sleep, not spent the past several hours inside a hot, crowded bar.

There were plenty of things she didn't understand about this mysterious stranger. How had he been able to deduce so easily that she was on the run? How was he able to see inside her and to make her feel so damned safe and protected?

He claimed to be an ordinary businessman on a routine business trip, but he was clearly much more than that. Whatever, he had given her a valuable gift the last two nights, the gift of peace of mind, however fleeting it may have been.

"I usually ask one of the bouncers to walk me to my car after work . . ."

Harry smiled. "Well, there's not much point in that, is there? It just so happens that I'm on my way out also."

They turned toward the door and Victoria said, "Thanks again for the drinks, and for being such a great listener and for . . . well . . . for everything, I guess."

The stranger chuckled as they walked into the cooling desert night. Victoria shivered, partly from the abrupt change in temperature and partly from something else. "Believe me," he said.

"Thanks are totally unnecessary. It wasn't much of a sacrifice to spend the evening in the company of a beautiful woman, listening to the best jazz piano I've ever heard."

They reached a dark-colored Chevy Caprice and Harry said, "This is my rental. Where's your car?" He seemed entirely unsurprised when she nodded at the little Pontiac Sunbird right next to the Chevy.

"Well," she said, feeling herself tensing, her stomach muscles beginning to clench in fear as it became clear they were about to part ways, "I know you said I shouldn't thank you, but I have to. You have no idea how much it means to me to experience at least a little taste of normalcy, even if it was for only a few hours. It was a precious gift and something I won't soon forget."

"About that," Harry replied, turning to face Victoria. He took her right hand in both of his, as he had done earlier. She felt herself tense up involuntarily but forced herself not to pull away.

He waited, saying nothing, until she looked up into his eyes. The moon was behind him, his face indistinct in the shadows. "Listen to me for a minute," he said, "and don't answer until I've finished."

Victoria cocked her head, confused. "Um . . . okay."

"You said you saw Stark here in Vegas a couple of days ago. The fact that he's here means he probably knows specifically where you live, and if he doesn't already, he'll find out soon enough. You're apartment is where he'll make a move for you when he decides it's time. His obsession is telling him to relive that night in Manhattan, meaning your home is where you're most vulnerable."

Victoria's knees weakened. She felt her mouth go dry. She pictured Joel Stark waiting for her in her parking lot at the Royal Flush.

Harry reached out and took her other hand, enfolding both of hers inside his. "I'm not trying to frighten you, but I want you to know you have an option. My motel is just a short distance from here. I know we just met, but I want to help you, and the fact is you desperately *need* someone's help. I understand you have no reason to trust me, but I'm asking you to do just that. Stay in my motel room tonight. Stark will have no clue where you are, and you'll get some much-needed rest."

Victoria hesitated, wanting badly to be able to trust this man who made her feel so safe. It had been so long since she had put her trust in anyone besides herself that she wasn't sure she even knew how, but the thought of disappearing, even for one night, to a hideaway off Joel Stark's radar was incredibly tempting.

"I'll bring you there and get you settled in," Harry continued, "and then I need to go out for a little while. You'll have the place all to yourself. It'll be cozy and quiet and safe, and when I come back I'll sack out on the floor. Then, in the morning, when you're fresh and rested, we'll sit down over a cup of coffee and take another look at your situation. Maybe things won't seem quite so hopeless after a good night's sleep."

Victoria envisioned her poorly lit parking lot, deserted at this time of the night. She considered what Harry said about Stark planning to attack her there. It made sense when he said it.

But what finally made her mind up for her was the sudden realization that if this man, Harry Carson, meant her harm, he could easily have forced her into his car and driven off ten times in the last ten minutes. No one would ever have known.

She took a deep breath and jumped off the cliff. "A good night's sleep sounds wonderful. I sort of remember what that's like and I wouldn't mind reliving it, even if it's only for one night."

Harry opened the passenger door and ushered her inside, then circled around the front of the car. Victoria could see him scanning the mostly empty lot as he walked. It didn't look to her like any of the cars were occupied, but the night was so dark and the shadows so complete under the sodium arc lamps that it was impossible to tell.

When he opened the driver's door and slid behind the wheel, Victoria asked, "You have to go out? At two o'clock in the morning? What could you possibly be doing at this time of night, even in Vegas?"

Harry grinned at her and she decided it made him look ten years younger. "Vegas never sleeps, right? That's what I've heard, anyway."

He took in the expression on her face and laughed softly. "I've just got a few errands to run, and it's a lot easier to do while everyone else is sleeping off their margaritas and cosmopolitans and dreaming about winning their money back than it is when they're driving around, clogging up my streets."

The Chevy pulled smoothly out of the lot and Victoria leaned against the door. She wanted to make conversation, if only to be polite to this man who was being so kind to her, but the stress of the last few days was catching up with her. She was exhausted.

She struggled to keep her eyes open as Harry drove. He had said his motel was right down the road, but he seemed to be making random turns, even backtracking once or twice. She realized he was being careful, making sure they weren't being followed.

Then her eyes closed and she was out.

* * *

Jack nosed the Caprice into the spot directly in front of his room and killed the engine. His passenger must be even more tired than he had thought, because she didn't awaken when he opened his door and the Caprice's interior lights came on.

He crossed to the other side of the vehicle and eased the passenger door open, reaching to support her as she began to slide out of the car. The sudden motion awoke her, and she blinked and shook her head, gasping in a burst of initial panic before looking up and recognizing Jack.

"Easy," he said softly. "We're at my motel. Let's get you inside so you can sleep."

He helped her into his room and moved to the small dresser while she sat on the bed, clearly uncomfortable with the situation. He hadn't brought much extra clothing, but pulled out a pair of shorts he had slept in last night and a clean T-shirt, tossing them to the beautiful musician. "It's not much," he said with a smile, "but it's better than sleeping in a tux."

"Thank you," she murmured after a yawn. Then she disappeared into the bathroom to change. When she emerged a couple of minutes later, she looked tiny in Jack's clothes, despite being quite tall.

While she was changing clothes, Jack had pulled down the bedcovers. "I promise no one will bother you here," he said. "Get some rest, and I'll be back before you know it. I'll try to be quiet when I return, and when you wake up, I'll be sleeping right in front of the door."

Victoria shook her head. "I can't take your bed. It's not right."

Jack chuckled. "Don't worry about it. I've slept on much worse than a motel room floor. I'll be fine, believe me."

She shook her head again and he thought she was going to protest more. Then she sighed and slid under the blankets, pulling them up to her chin. "Thank you so much," she said and closed her eyes.

"You're very welcome," Jack answered. Then he slipped out the door, locking it behind him, and went to work.

22

Blake Standiford was playing blackjack.

Drunk.

It was a dangerous combination, stupid really. He knew that but didn't care. He was struggling mightily with the notion that just because some pushy bitch had gotten herself killed—which was no more than she deserved—he now was being forced to pack up and leave the town in which he had been born and raised and had lived his entire life.

It wasn't fucking fair.

So Blake was angry. He was also a little scared. He hated to admit it, even if only to himself, but he was beginning to feel that little tingle up and down the back of his neck that told him time was running out. Big Tony had bought his bullshit story about having nothing to do with Kathy Saldana's death, he knew that much.

But just because he had bought the lie this morning didn't mean things couldn't change. The fact of the matter was that things *would* change, and fast, once Sammy Saldana got past his shock and grief over Kathy's death and started wondering why the hell she had been spending so much time in Vegas in the first place.

And who she had been spending it with.

When that happened, Sammy would send a crew down here to investigate, and when *that* happened, Blake knew he would be toast. He had done nothing to hide his relationship with Sammy's woman, reveling in the bad-boy notoriety it had provided. In retrospect, flaunting the fact that he was screwing Kathy had been a monumentally bad idea, but long-range planning had never been Blake Standiford's strong suit.

Thus, the reality was clear: it was critical he be out of Vegas before Shotgun Sammy's boys arrived. That reality sucked, but sucking didn't make it any less true.

There was one problem, though, and it was a big one. He needed scratch. Blake had never started a brand-new life before, but he had a pretty good handle on the value of money and he knew it would take cash, lots of cash, for him to do so while continuing to live the lifestyle he deserved. His plan had been to clean out a petty cash account kept for Mercadante family insider use, but upon his trip to the bank this afternoon, Blake had discovered the account closed, the funds transferred.

And that was a very bad sign.

Tony wouldn't have closed the account for no reason. The reason may have had nothing to do with Blake, that was certainly possible, but if that were the case, why wouldn't Tony have mentioned it? Told him how to access the new account?

It all added up to trouble, and when Blake Arthur Standiford III got nervous or angry, he drank. That had always been the case and tonight was no different.

He scanned his cards. A seven and a nine, with the dealer showing queen. Total shit, just like he had been getting all night. He sipped his whiskey and water and glowered at the dealer out of habit while he considered his options. Fat Tony may have shut off Blake's access to the Mercadante family's petty cash, but after a little serious thinking, Blake had come up with a backup plan.

It would be risky, but it might work. And if it did, Blake figured he would have all the money he would need for a long time. A massive drug deal was going down tomorrow afternoon south of Vegas. Heroin, being trucked up from South America. Mercadante's organization was poised to rake in over a hundred grand in cash, all of it untraceable by the authorities and, even more importantly, by Big Tony Mercadante, should it go missing.

Blake hoped he would draw the assignment of making the exchange. Whether that would happen or not would probably depend on whether Tony still trusted him. Blake figured it was a tossup at this point.

But if he *did* draw the assignment, it would be a simple thing to make the transfer, then put two 9mm slugs into the head of whatever other Mercadante guy had been assigned to accompany him. Then he'd simply dump his partner's body in the desert and take off. He would be three hundred miles away before Big Tony even knew he was gone.

And if he didn't draw the assignment?

That would complicate things considerably, but Blake would adjust. He knew by heart the route the Mercadante family drivers would take to get to the exchange location. He should, he had driven it plenty of times. Blake would simply wait outside town and hijack the assholes with the cash before they could make it to the exchange. He'd force them off the road, put bullets in their heads in the ensuing confusion, then grab the cash and run.

It was risky but doable.

And what was more, Blake had no choice.

He became aware of the dealer making impatient grumbling noises and took a hit on his seven-nine and, predictably, busted. He was well aware it was a mistake to gamble—or to make life-and-death decisions, for that matter—while half-trashed, but fuck it. Even drunk, Blake Arthur Standiford III was smarter and sharper than just about anyone in Big Tony's employ.

As far as the cards were concerned, they would turn around eventually. They always did. There was only one thing to do: wait it out until your luck changed.

Two things, he corrected himself. *Wait out the cards and get another drink.* A gorgeous waitress dressed in the requisite short skirt and tight blouse wandered by and Blake grabbed her, literally, getting a handful of young female ass.

She squirmed away, whirling and staring daggers at him, and immediately, seemingly out of nowhere, a bouncer appeared. He was big and strong and ill-tempered, but Blake knew he could make mincemeat out of the pussy if he wanted to.

The musclehead placed himself between the waitress and Blake and said, "Touch one of our girls again and I'll break your fucking arm, got it?"

Blake returned the kid's stare, humiliated now as well as angry and drunk and worried about his situation with Big Tony. The bouncer was definitely a juicer; his arms looked like a pair of oak trees had sprouted from his shoulders.

Blake didn't care. He sneered at the kid and said, "You have no fucking idea who you're talking to, pal. Do yourself a favor and get lost."

"I know exactly who you are, little man. Big Tony says I have his personal permission to break you in half any time I want. So *you* do *yourself* a favor and stop harassing the girls, before I decide now is that time." Oak Tree spun on his heel and strutted away, disappearing into the crowd like he had been a mirage.

Red-faced and furious, Blake threw his cards onto the table and leapt to his feet. He bumped into a man walking by and snarled, "Watch where you're fucking going," and the man opened his mouth to reply but then slammed it shut and kept walking.

"Fuck this," Blake muttered as he stalked through the casino. He didn't need aggravation from some snot-nosed little prick who thought he was king of the world just because he had been given the authority to push people around.

He weaved and wobbled as he headed to his car, drunker than he had realized, angrier than he had probably ever been without then killing someone. He ran his humiliation at the hands of the muscle-bound twenty-something gorilla over and over in his mind, getting more and more pissed off as he did.

So Big Fat Tony had given some half-wit bouncer permission to keep him in line. Him! Blake Arthur Standiford III! Blake hadn't even been aware that Big Tony knew he liked to drink and gamble here, but obviously Tony knew more about his people than Blake had ever given him credit for.

Well, so what? Maybe after stealing all of that drug money tomorrow, Blake would drive into Vegas and spread Fat Tony's brains all over his shabby office before hitting the road for good. He'd force the dumb fuck to squirm and beg for his life, drag it out a good long while, and then he'd bury two slugs in Tony's ear.

It was a satisfying daydream, and Blake ran variations of it through his head as he stumbled to his car and drove through the Nevada night. He knew he shouldn't be driving after all of that whiskey, but fuck it. If a cop stopped him, he'd blow the unlucky fucker's head off and drive away.

But no cops stopped him. He didn't see so much as a single cruiser on the way home, and before he knew it, he had arrived back in his quiet little neighborhood, tired and drunk and ready for bed.

23

Victoria rarely made it through an entire night without dreaming. And those dreams were almost always nightmares, inevitably involving Joel Stark, horrifying vignettes of him raping her, cutting her, torturing her. Killing her. She often woke herself up screaming, shaking and sweaty, the covers twisted around her trembling body.

Tonight, though, was different. Tonight there were no nightmares. Tonight her dreams starred not Joel Stark but Harry Carson. And in those dreams, Harry flew out of the sky on a magnificent white-winged stallion, landing in the parking lot of the Royal Flush Apartments. He climbed down off his stallion and beat Joel Stark with his bare hands.

Then he pulled Victoria astride the horse, setting her behind him. Then they lifted into the air, the two of them soaring high above Las Vegas, whisking her away and removing the terror from her life forever.

24

Jack had long since come to grips with the odd hours demanded by his profession. Sipping coffee at Tequila Mockingbird, driving the piano player to his motel room after closing time, and then going off to work at two-thirty in the morning was no big deal for him because he had been doing most of his work while the rest of the world slept for over a decade and a half.

He had to admit, though, that he was tiring of these late-night hours, but he *was* used to them.

Victoria had told him the name of her apartment complex while they were chatting on one of her breaks at Tequila Mockingbird, and after programming the address into his portable GPS—a low-end model he had received from Mr. Stanton before leaving on this mission that would be smashed and then discarded in a random Dumpster before he left Nevada—Jack wound his way south out of Las Vegas toward Overton.

Traffic was light, although the streets were far from deserted. He stopped at a twenty-four-hour liquor store inside the Vegas city limits and bought a fifth of cheap whiskey and then continued on his way. As he drove, Jack tried to piece together what he had learned about Joel Stark from the terrified musician currently fast asleep in his bed.

He had no doubt she was telling the truth as she knew it. The young woman was sincere and honest to a fault, Jack could already see that. But more than anything else, she was clearly caught in the grip of a gut-wrenching terror that took precedence over everything else in her life. He doubted she could have made up a believable lie about Stark right now even if she wanted to. Survival was her priority.

It seemed a safe bet to Jack to assume that Stark had just arrived in the Las Vegas area when Victoria happened to see him a couple of days ago. His history had been one of rash action where she was concerned, which made sense given the nature of his obsession combined with his clearly sociopathic personality. Based on everything Victoria had said about Stark, Jack doubted the man had the ability to control his obsession for more than forty-eight to seventy-two hours.

If all of that was true—and that was big "if," Jack knew—then he thought he might have come up with a reasonable solution to her problem, and one that would tie in well with his own reasons for being in Vegas.

And if not, if his analysis of Victoria's longtime stalker was off the mark, all he would have wasted was a few hours of his time over the course of a couple of nights. It was a chance worth taking, because it seemed clear that the young red-haired musician was approaching her breaking point.

Jack entered the main parking lot of the Royal Flush apartment complex and immediately turned away from Victoria's building. The complex consisted of a series of large rectangular structures, each containing six apartments, built in a pattern designed to look random, to give the appearance of a neighborhood that had grown up haphazardly over time.

The reality, of course, was just the opposite. The entire complex had undoubtedly been constructed at once. But the access road connecting the parking lots for each of the buildings meandered in a long, winding semicircle, allowing Jack to cruise slowly behind all of the buildings and eventually approach Victoria's apartment from a direction opposite the main entrance.

He turned into the lot reserved for the building next to Victoria's. Killed his headlights. Eased into an open space under a shade tree and smiled. The location was perfect. He could see not just the entrance to Victoria's building, but halfway down one side as well.

He settled in his seat and stifled a yawn. Checked his watch.

It was just after three a.m. He guessed Stark would have staked out Victoria's apartment almost immediately following his arrival, based on the level of obsession that would make a man stalk a terrified young woman across the country. It was only a guess, though. There was no real way of knowing how long the man had been in the city when Victoria spotted him.

If he was right, though, Jack thought there was at least a decent chance Stark would be back tonight to execute his plan.

And when he did, he would encounter a little surprise.

Jack hoped he wasn't too late, that Stark hadn't already come and gone. He didn't think that would be the case, though. Stark would know Victoria's schedule, which meant he would be aware that she worked until Tequila Mockingbird's two a.m. closing time.

He would give her plenty of time to get out of work, drive home, and get into bed. He would want to make sure she was fast asleep before breaking in and reintroducing himself to her, which meant there was almost no way Stark would show up before three-thirty at the earliest, maybe closer to four.

If he was reading Stark right, a questionable proposition at best.

He sipped a coffee that had started out bitter and hot but was now bitter and lukewarm. He grimaced and swallowed, then took another sip and repeated the process. His gaze scanned the building as he passed the time by trying to puzzle out exactly how someone with Joel Stark's obvious psychopathy had had the technical expertise to track the object of his obsession around the country, not just once, but several times.

Victoria hadn't made things particularly difficult for him. She had kept her name, and worse, had made a living as an entertainer under that name. Still, Jack doubted Stark was operating alone. More likely he had a friend or relative in a position of authority somewhere. The police maybe, or the FBI, or some other federal agency with access to citizens' private records.

Jack was determined to ensure the cycle of terror being propagated by the remorseless Joel Stark ended here.

Tonight, if possible.

He took another sip of his coffee—still bitter, now even colder—and continued to scan the area, his eyes in constant motion.

25

Joel was sick and tired of waiting. Tomorrow would be his third day here in Vegas and he hated it. Hated the never-ending stream of tourists clogging the strip, hated the relentless heat blasting down day after day, hated knowing his little princess was so close but he had yet to enjoy her.

He had demonstrated to his own satisfaction that he was capable of taking things slowly and methodically. He had developed a plan and had stuck to it, following the beautiful redhead to work, learning her schedule, watching her without allowing her to see him *and* without giving in to the urge to stuff her into the trunk of his car and take off.

He was proud of himself. He had even examined his princess's apartment building—from the outside, of course—last night while she slept. It was torture knowing she was just a few feet away, on the other side of the exterior wall, likely nearly naked and ripe for the taking. But he had maintained his resolve, forcing himself to retreat, going over his plans one more time by the light of day.

He had done everything necessary to ensure that he would finally be successful. And now it was time to act, before he did something stupid and alerted her to his presence, as he had done so many times before.

Joel parked his rusting piece of shit car in the lot of a dry cleaning establishment that looked as though it had passed its heyday when Bugsy Siegel was running things in Vegas. The shop was one of the few remaining businesses still making a go of it in a beaten-down strip mall located no more than a quarter mile from the Royal Flush apartments. Returning to pick up the car would be a little inconvenient when the time came to get the hell out of Dodge, but there was no way he was going to take the chance of someone noticing a vehicle that didn't belong in Victoria's lot and then alerting the police about it when the girl turned up missing.

The logistics of getting Victoria into the car would be tricky but were doable. It was all part of his plan. After the day or so they would spend getting reacquainted inside the apartment, Joel would simply tie her up securely, duct-tape a couple of socks inside her mouth to keep her quiet, and then hike back and retrieve his car. He would park outside a different building—slightly risky but not overly so—and then sneak Victoria out to it at three or four in the morning.

Simple. Now that he had seen the light and understood the value of caution and of taking the time to do things right, Joel knew this time he would not fail. He would finally get what he had craved for so long.

He walked along the side of the road, being careful not to move so quickly he would attract attention, not that anyone was around at this time of night in this part of Overton. On the rare occasions a car approached, he slinked into the shadows and waited for it to pass. It wouldn't do to have a suspicious cop brace him and then remember him later.

Careful and easy.

Even with his slow progress, Joel arrived at the grounds of the complex in less than fifteen minutes. The place was a ghost town, the three-thirty a.m. darkness broken only by the flickering watery yellow of unevenly spaced light poles, totally ineffective against the partially overcast desert night.

He moved quietly along the edge of the Royal Flush property line, approaching Victoria's apartment from behind. He slipped into a small grove of scrub trees and leaned against one, eyeing his princess's building for any signs of activity.

Nothing. And why would there be? Even night owls like Victoria had long since gone to bed. He fingered the glass cutter in the pocket of his windbreaker. It was long and thin, shaped like a pencil, with a securely capped, razor-sharp blade at one end. He knew he would need it to gain access to his girl's apartment, since undoubtedly her days of leaving bedroom windows unlocked and accessible were long gone.

He waited five minutes, and when the time passed with no activity he waited five more, just to convince himself he could and to reinforce his determination that this time things would be different.

Finally he broke cover, easing out of the clump of trees and moving to the side of the apartment building. A row of poorly maintained ornamental shrubs ran along the side of the building, scraggly and dying. Joel slipped through a small opening, presumably made over the years by the groundskeepers, and flattened himself against the stucco wall.

He was now right next to Victoria's window. His princess was just a few feet away, waiting for him, and despite his determination to take things slowly, he was shaking with anticipation and he knew there was no holding back any longer.

He pulled the glass cutter from his pocket and flipped off the plastic sheath covering its blade. Lifted it to the window and began scribing an arc on the glass. It hissed softly in the dry desert air. He slid the cutter slowly, smoothly, across the surface, absorbed in his work.

26

Jack came instantly alert at the motion, sensed more than seen, in the vicinity of a clump of trees that had been planted behind and between two of the apartment buildings. He sat up in his seat and leaned forward, squinting against the darkness.

It was a person, dressed in dark clothing, almost certainly a man. The figure moved with a stealthy sense of purpose in a direct line toward a row of sick-looking shrubs separating the sides of the two buildings.

Jack was up and moving before the figure disappeared from view behind the shrubs. This had to be Stark. If it wasn't, it was the unluckiest cat burglar in the history of petty crime.

Jack slipped out of his car and eased the door mostly closed, leaving it slightly ajar to avoid the telltale *clunk.* He trotted across a small swale separating the parking lots, pulling Blake Standiford's Walther P22 out of the back of his jeans as he ran.

The little pistol held ten rounds fully loaded, which it was. The German-manufactured weapon was light and maneuverable, with a black polymer grip and a length of just over six inches. Its serial number had been filed off—not surprising considering where Jack had gotten it—but even if the serial number had still been on the gun it wouldn't have changed anything, since there was no way it could be traced back to him.

He reached the entrance to Victoria's building in seconds and moved to the corner, holding the Walther loosely in his right hand. Then he crouched down on all fours to present as small a target as possible and crawled past the two-foot opening between the shrubs and the side of the building.

Stark was standing a good thirty feet down, next to the window that presumably would open to Victoria's bedroom. At that distance and in the darkness, unless Stark was looking directly toward the front of the building—highly unlikely, given his obsession—Jack knew the man would never see him.

A second later he had crawled past the opening and stood. Followed the shrubs, estimating the distance as he went. When he reached a point he guessed put him directly behind Stark, Jack stopped and discovered a small opening in the tangle of arbor.

This was where Stark had entered. It had to be.

He eased through the gap, moving slowly, Walther pointed at the ground. Stark was there, his back turned, all his attention on the window, against which his right hand was pressed.

Jack raised the pistol and jammed it against the base of the man's skull. "You can live or you can die," he growled, his voice soft and low. "It all depends on how you approach the next few seconds."

Stark froze and everything stopped. The night was utterly, eerily silent.

"Good decision," Jack said. "Now, turn around very slowly."

The man pivoted and as he did, Jack noticed too late the glass cutter in his raised right hand, glittering in a splash of weak light from the parking lot. Stark slashed downward, aiming at Jack's eyes, and he jerked his head backward reflexively.

He was a split-second too slow. The surgical steel blade bit into Jack's skin under his eye, slicing nearly to the cheekbone in a thick splash of blood.

He reacted instantly, pivoting his wrist and pistol-whipping the thug with the butt of the Walther, driving his arm forward as his momentum took him backward. The blow was a glancing one, clipping off the side of Stark's skull, but it stunned the man and he staggered. Jack struck again with the weapon and this time the rapist dropped to the ground with a soft moan.

The entire fight took just seconds and played out in near-total silence. Jack stood with one hand clamped to his bleeding cheek. He was breathing heavily, more from adrenaline than from exertion.

He considered the prone form of Joel Stark, groaning quietly and twitching in the hard-packed dirt. It was tempting to sink a bullet in Stark's head right here and now and put an end to Victoria Welling's problems for good, but Jack controlled the impulse.

He had other plans for this monster.

The pain began to ratchet up in his face. The injury was bleeding profusely and burned like someone had inserted a lit blowtorch under the skin. Jack knew it was going to get worse before it got better. He ignored it.

Stark moaned again and began to roll to his feet and Jack kicked him once in the chest, hard, and the man went down again in a heap.

Jack dropped to his knees next to the dusty, dirty Stark and noted with satisfaction that the rapist was bleeding from the head where he had been struck with the Walther. The blood wasn't flowing quite as freely as it was from Jack's face, but he knew Stark couldn't be feeling too chipper right now, either. *Good. Serves him right.*

He picked the glass cutter off the ground where the man had dropped it.

Waited for the rapist's eyes to flutter open.

Seconds later they did, and he said, "Get your sorry ass up," his voice quiet but filled with menace.

Stark stumbled heavily to his feet. His eyes were glazed and he shook his head as if to clear the cobwebs, then he stared at Jack with a look of pure malevolence. "Who in the fuck are you?"

"I'm the guy who decides whether you live or die. And so far, you haven't earned many points in your favor. Now, start walking."

Stark bent and brushed dust and dirt off his clothes. He seemed pretty wobbly and Jack was glad. It might keep him from getting any more dangerous ideas. On the other hand, it was obvious he was stalling, probably hoping his head would clear enough to enable him to come at Jack again.

It was time to demonstrate the pecking order. He jammed the gun into the back of Stark's neck. "Start walking. I'm not going to tell you again."

The man stumbled forward a couple of steps and then spread his hands. "Where?"

"Away from an innocent woman's window would be a good start." He shoved Stark roughly forward and the two men trudged along the side of the building. A moment later they emerged from behind the shrubs next to the front door. Jack gestured to the right with the gun and they crossed the parking lot at an angle.

Back at his car, Jack held the weapon steady on his prisoner as he reached into the back seat and grabbed two plastic zip ties. Blood streamed down his face and his cheek throbbed, daggers of pain racing through his head with every beat of his heart.

"On your knees," he said quietly. "Hurry up." Despite the hour and the shadows enveloping his car, there was no time to waste. He didn't think anyone would see much if they happened to peek out an apartment window, but if some early riser walked out the front door of the building behind them on his way to work, there would be no way to mask what was happening here.

Stark dropped to his knees on the pavement, moving with obvious reluctance and no faster now than he had been before. Jack supposed he couldn't blame him. From Stark's perspective there was no upside in hurrying things along.

But Stark's perspective wasn't the one he cared about, and he bent and zipped the plastic ties quickly around Stark's wrists after forcing the man's hands behind his back. Then he pulled the rapist roughly to his feet and shoved him into the vehicle.

It took maybe two seconds to hurry around to the other side, and then Jack climbed into the car, fired it up, and began rolling toward the exit. Stark had remained utterly silent since their terse exchange at the side of Victoria's building, but now he said, "You're obviously no cop. What the hell's going on here?"

Jack ignored the question. Instead he asked, "Where'd you park you car?"

"Why would I tell you anything?"

"Because I have a gun and you don't." Jack had been weaving the vehicle slowly through the Royal Flush's serpentine access roads, and now he eased to a stop and turned to face Joel Stark. He lifted Blake Standiford's Walther and pressed the barrel lightly against Stark's forehead. "I suggest you remember that."

Stark squeezed his eyes shut, as if afraid this lunatic sitting on the other side of the car might just blow his brains out right here and now. A second passed, and then two, and then he reopened his eyes in seeming surprise at the realization he wasn't dead yet.

Jack lowered the gun and turned his attention back to the access road. He hoped the blood leaking out of each of them was being trapped by the clear plastic tarp he had placed over the bench seats before leaving the Tumbling Dice motel, but there was nothing he could do about it now.

The interior was quiet, the only sound the low hum of the Chevy's engine. Jack glanced at his captive and saw an oily grin slide across Stark's pockmarked face.

"Ahhh. . . . I know what's going on here," his captive said, amusement obvious in his voice. "You must be the little slut's boyfriend."

"She's no slut. She's just a normal young woman, or at least she was until you raped her and terrorized her and sent her running in fear across the country. What the hell is wrong with you?"

It was as if Jack hadn't spoken. Stark's taunting smile never faltered, and he mockingly said, "Guess I owe you an apology, lover boy. Now that she's had me, you can't satisfy her, can you? You're not enough for her, am I right?"

Cat-quick, Jack leaned right and slammed the barrel of the Walther into Stark's throat, and the man began coughing and gagging as the side of his head bounced off the passenger window.

"Let's get something straight right now," Jack hissed. "You're nothing more to me than a cockroach, one who deserves to be stomped underfoot. If you weren't such a limp-dick pervert, you wouldn't have to break into women's apartments just to get one to pay attention to you. One more word about Victoria and I'm going to shoot your dick off, do you understand? Nod if you understand, pervert."

Rage and humiliation smoldered in Stark's eyes, but after a moment he nodded slowly, still coughing and wheezing and struggling to breathe.

"Now," Jack continued. "Last chance. Tell me where your car's parked or I kill you right here and bury your worthless carcass in the desert. Your choice. It doesn't make a damned bit of difference to me either way."

Stark's eyes searched Jack's face. Apparently decided he was serious. "Take a right at the exit. I'm a little ways down on the left, in a dry cleaner's parking lot."

Jack reached into the back seat, picked up a towel and pressed it to his face. Keeping firm pressure against the gash, he put the car back in gear and accelerated toward the exit. Turned right as instructed and pulled onto the deserted road.

Stark cleared his throat and said, "I don't know why I bothered to answer your question. You're going to kill me anyway."

"What makes you think that?"

"You're not going to kill me?"

"I didn't say that, either." Ahead and to the left, a small, beaten-down strip mall loomed, the storefronts appearing to be split between businesses struggling to survive and those that had already succumbed to the pressures of a down economy, even in a town like Vegas.

Jack turned to Stark, who had slumped uncomfortably back in his seat, his body pressing his cuffed hands against the seat back. He gestured with his head out the window. "This it?"

"Yeah, this is it." All fight seemed to have gone out of the man, but that might be nothing more than a conscious effort on his part to get Jack to let his guard down. That wasn't going to happen.

Jack doused his headlights and drove into the lot. An ancient Monte Carlo of indeterminate color was parked in front of a tired-looking dry cleaning establishment. The car was pocked with rust and dented in dozens of places. Jack pulled to a stop next to it.

Stark's nervousness seemed to have spiked again now that they had entered the lot. The uneasy status quo was about to change and he knew it. "What happens now?"

"Get out," Jack said, as he lifted a skinny paper bag and a small first aid kit out of the back seat.

"Then what?" For the first time, Stark's voice wavered.

"Then we change cars. We're taking yours the rest of the way."

"The rest of the way where?"

"Shut up and move."

27

"Where are you staying?" Jack asked the question without taking his eyes from the road. He was surprised to discover that despite the Monte Carlo's decrepit appearance it actually felt solid and drove reasonably well.

Stark looked into Jack's eyes with a mixture of contempt and acceptance. "You're bleeding all over my car."

Jack had dropped the towel into his lap while he drove, and now he pressed it back to his face. He did his best to ignore the pain, which was throbbing with the bright intensity of a fresh knife wound. "There," he said. "Is that better? I'd hate to damage the interior of such a beautiful machine."

Stark said nothing and when it became clear he had no intention of continuing the conversation, Jack leaned over and pressed Standiford's Walther to Stark's forehead as he had done before.

"Where are you staying?" he asked again, speaking slowly and quietly. "You know the drill. Tell me now or die."

"Cactus Motel." Stark spit the words out like razor blades after a moment's hesitation.

Jack said, "Okay. I'm going to slice the zip ties off your wrists, and you're going to reach into your pocket and hand me your car keys. If anything besides a set of keys comes out of that pocket, I'm going to shoot you in the face. If you move a muscle in any way I don't like, I'm going to shoot you in the face. If you look at me cross-eyed, I'm going to shoot you in the face. Understand where I'm going with this?"

Stark narrowed his eyes and Jack thought he was going to say something, but he kept his mouth shut and nodded. Jack pulled a small pocketknife out of his pocket with his left hand while holding the gun steadily on Stark with his right. Then he gestured with his head and Stark leaned to the side. A moment later his hands were free.

"Get the key," Jack said, replacing the knife in his pocket.

Stark slid one filthy hand into the right pocket of his jeans. Pulled out a single key and handed it to Jack.

A moment later the car was running and Jack said, "Very good. Guide me to the Cactus Motel and don't do anything stupid. I assume even someone of your limited intellectual capacity hasn't forgotten already what will happen if you do something stupid."

Hatred smoldered in Stark's eyes but he did as he was told, and less than five minutes later they had arrived at a rundown establishment whose better days, if they had ever existed at all, were long gone. Jack was unsurprised to discover Victoria's stalker was staying so close to her home. She was, after all, the reason the man had driven nearly three thousand miles across the country.

The motel featured an office with a flickering neon sign in the window that read, TEL, the "M" and the "O" having burnt out, probably years ago. More significant than the sign, though, was the fact that the motel office was dark, meaning the desk clerk was probably sacked out in the back somewhere. If that was the case, the likelihood of him suddenly getting up from his slumber and peering into the parking lot was slim.

There was no way of knowing how many of the other Cactus Motel rooms were in use at the moment, but the lot was sparsely populated with cars. Hopefully any guests who *were* here and who were still up at this hour would be too drunk or drugged-up to notice—or care—that another guest was being held captive by a man bleeding from his face into a towel.

Jack followed Stark's instructions, easing the Monte Carlo to a stop in front of a room located almost as far from the office as was possible. He killed the engine and pocketed the keys and said, "You know how we play this game. Don't yell or do anything else to draw attention to yourself. If you do I'll kill you. And don't think for a second I'd hesitate to put a bullet in your back if you try to run. Tell me you understand."

Stark's gaze bored in on Jack. His hatred was palpable. After a second he said grudgingly, "I understand."

"Then let's go. Walk straight to your door, unlock it and step inside. I'll be right behind you, so don't bother trying to jump in and slam the door before I can follow."

Jack dropped the bloody towel on the floor and picked up the paper bag he had brought with him. Then he opened his door and stepped out of the car quickly, slipping the gun into his pocket as he did. It was highly unlikely anyone was looking out a window, but why take chances? On the other side of the Pontiac, Stark climbed out as well, scanning the parking lot. Jack could sense him looking for something, anything, he could use to turn the tables on his attacker.

But there was nothing.

The other cars in the motel lot were dark and silent, as were the dirty windows of the rooms they were parked outside. The flickering lamps hanging off ancient light poles did nothing to reassure guests of their nighttime safety, but they provided more light than Jack would need to pick off Stark should he try to run.

Jack waited patiently at the front of the car—he decided the color was probably purple, although even now he wouldn't have put money on it—while Joel Stark trudged toward his motel room, still in no hurry. He made it halfway and then stopped.

"What are you waiting for?" Jack said. "Move it."

"No. The minute we go inside that room, you're going to kill me. Why the hell would I do that?"

Jack leaned forward, holding Stark's cold gaze. When he spoke, he spoke quietly. "If I wanted you dead, you'd be lying in a pool of your own blood back at the Royal Flush Apartments. I didn't go to all the trouble and risk of bringing you here just to shoot you now."

Stark shook his head, his anger and frustration now joined by confusion. "Then what the hell are we doing here?"

Jack gripped the bottom of the paper bag with his gun hand, and with the other lifted a bottle of cheap whiskey by the neck, slipping it far enough out of the bag to display to Joel Stark.

Then he smiled. "We're gonna have a little party."

28

The inside of Stark's motel room was about what Jack had expected. Threadbare carpeting that looked as though it hadn't been vacuumed since the 1970's covering an uneven floor, with an unmade double bed taking up most of the room's interior. An ancient television set wobbled atop a scarred wooden writing desk. An iron pipe ran from ceiling to floor behind a freestanding lamp in one corner that provided barely enough light to dispel the darkness.

Stark moved a few feet inside the room and then stopped, back to Jack, shoulders drawn inward like he half-expected to take a bullet in the back. Jack let him think it.

He closed the door quietly and locked it. Eased over to the corner and stepped behind the floor lamp, Walther trained on Stark. Placed a hand on the pipe and yanked with all his strength.

The pipe didn't budge.

It was perfect. Jack only needed it to hold for a few minutes and it was clearly heavy enough and strong enough for that.

"Come here," he said to Stark, who turned around slowly. Reluctantly. He had been thrown for a loop by the sudden appearance of the bag with the whiskey in it. Jack was glad. A confused prisoner, off-guard and on edge, was a hell of a lot easier to control than a confident one.

Stark shuffled across the room and as he walked, Jack plucked another zip tie out of his pocket. He maintained a steady grip on the gun and kept it trained center mass on the prisoner as he approached. No man, no matter how quick, would be able to inflict any serious damage on Jack before he could squeeze off a gut shot, and at this point, confused and hurting from two blows to the head earlier, Joel Stark would hardly qualify as "quick."

Blood dripped in a steady patter onto the floor from Jack's facial wound. There would be no way to escape Vegas now without leaving behind his DNA and he hoped that wouldn't eventually turn into a problem. Stark was bleeding also, but if the rest of the night went the way Jack expected it to, the authorities would certainly follow up on where all the blood had come from.

It would not take them long to discover more than one person had been here tonight. The same was likely true of Stark's car.

One thing Jack had going for him was the fact that nowhere in the system was there any record of Jack Sheridan's DNA, nor of his fingerprints, nor of any other conventional form of identification. Those items had been wiped clean, eliminated from all U.S. Government databases the day he completed his military training for the unit so secret it didn't have a name.

In any event, now was not the time to worry about the DNA issue. Jack had more immediate concerns.

Stark approached slowly and Jack held up a hand. "That's far enough." He kept his voice cold and hard. "Hands around the pipe."

When Stark complied, Jack whipped the ties around his wrists, effectively handcuffing the man to the sturdy piece of iron.

"Don't move," he said—hopefully unnecessarily—and walked into the tiny bathroom. Among the detritus scattered over the worn laminate countertop was what he was looking for: a clear plastic drinking cup. He retrieved the cup and returned to the living area.

Picked up the whiskey bottle and poured until the cup was three-quarters full.

"Let's get this party started," he said, placing the cup in his prisoner's hands.

"What the fuck do you think you're doing?"

Jack lifted the Walther and displayed it to his prisoner, just in case he had forgotten where he fit in the hierarchy. "Drink," he said quietly.

Stark's confusion was evident as he brought the cup to his lips with shaking hands.

"That thing had better be empty when I come back," Jack said, turning and retracing his steps to the bathroom.

He squinted in the dirty light as he examined his injured cheek in the vanity mirror. The damage Stark had inflicted with his glass cutter looked relatively minor, although the wound was deep and had bled profusely. He had been slashed just below his eye, where there was nothing but skin and bone. Any cut in that location was bound to look worse than it really was.

The injury probably would require sutures, but that wasn't going to happen, at least not here in Vegas. He would patch himself up the best he could now and then revisit the situation back in New Hampshire when this job was finished.

Jack cleaned the area as thoroughly as he could, given the relative lack of supplies. He ignored the burning and throbbing in his cheek and accepted the fact that he would be dealing with discomfort for the remainder of the assignment.

All the more reason to get it over with and get the hell out of Dodge.

He patted his face dry with what looked like a relatively clean towel and although the gash continued to bleed, the flow had slowed to a sluggish ooze. He opened his first aid kit and removed a clean gauze pad and some tape. Secured the bandage. Decided he would live another day.

All of this was taking time Jack had not budgeted when planning the operation. If he was going to have any chance of accomplishing what he wanted to tonight, he needed to get moving. He left the bathroom and returned to Stark, who had apparently taken Jack's admonition to drink his whiskey to heart. The plastic cup was empty and since there was no place Stark could have dumped it without the evidence being plain to Jack, he had to have drunk it.

The rapist was now well on his way to becoming intoxicated. His face was flushed and slack and he sagged against the iron pipe like an alcoholic at closing time. It wasn't surprising, Jack thought, given the amount of liquor the cup had contained and the speed with which Stark had finished it. He would only become more impaired as the alcohol was absorbed into his system.

Jack refilled the cup to half its previous level and handed it once again to Stark. "Still thirsty?"

The prisoner tried to fix Jack with a glare, but he wasn't able to manage it. His eyes slid off Jack's face as he wobbled slightly. He accepted the cup and drank awkwardly, lowering his face next to the pipe and straining with his zip-tied hands to bring the whiskey to his lips.

While he was drinking, Jack gathered his things together—including the towel he had used on his injury and the bag containing the whiskey—and slipped on a pair of surgical gloves. He wiped down everything he had touched in the bathroom and then returned to Stark. He sliced through the zip ties and placed them carefully in his pocket.

"Time to go," he said, smiling tightly.

"What the hell is going on here?" Stark said. Jack thought he did a reasonable job of not slurring his words, considering how much liquor he had just consumed in a very short time.

"What's going on is that this party is over. It's time to hit the road and pay someone a visit."

"Pay someone a visit? Who?"

"You'll see."

29

Blake was still seething an hour after arriving home. His plan had been to fall into bed immediately—tomorrow would be a big day, maybe the biggest of his life, and he needed to be on top of his game if he expected to survive—but that plan hadn't taken into account being pushed around and humiliated by some asshole hopped up on steroids.

The first thing he did after parking his Mercedes in the garage was wobble into the living room, yank open the glass door to his liquor cabinet, and mix a drink. Another mistake, probably, but Blake knew there was no way he would be able to sleep until he calmed down.

Let it go. He was a stupid punk kid and you're gonna be leaving this city of whores and losers forever tomorrow anyway. Just let it go.

But that was easier said than done, and one drink turned into two, and then three as he watched SportsCenter on his big-screen TV and fingered a gun, one of many he had hidden throughout his home. He fantasized about blowing Big Tony's brains out as well as the punk bouncer's, a two-for-one deal on his way out of town. It was a satisfying mental movie, and gradually his simmering anger melted away into a kind of self-satisfied exhaustion.

He glanced at the clock hanging over his TV, a diamond-encrusted, ostentatious monstrosity that had been given to him by a guy whose wife he had killed a few years ago as a favor. The fucking thing looked as though it belonged in Liberace's house, it was that goddamned ugly, but the guy's heart had been in the right place and so Blake had stuck it on the wall despite its unattractiveness. The gift had meant something to him.

Right now, though, what it meant was that the time had disappeared, evaporating like dew on a desert morning. Blake's eyes widened as he stared at the clock and through his drunken fog tried to decipher the meaning of the hands on its ugly face.

It was three a.m.

It couldn't possibly be three a.m.

He blinked. Looked again. It remained three a.m.

Holy shit. It's three a.m.

He struggled to his feet, weaving and bobbing like Muhammad Ali rope-a-doping Joe Frazier, and staggered upstairs to his bedroom, where he fell fully clothed into bed, his weapon still in his hand.

He was asleep within seconds.

30

By the time they arrived in Blake Standiford's North Las Vegas neighborhood it was nearly four-thirty a.m., later than Jack had planned for and not long before the area's early risers would start getting out of their houses and on the road to begin their workdays. There was no time to spare.

Stark was by now blind drunk, which was exactly the way Jack wanted him. The rapist had gotten past his initial confusion and skepticism about why his captor would go to the trouble of ambushing him only to ply him with alcohol, embracing the idea wholeheartedly the more he drank, swigging whiskey from his plastic cup during the ride across town.

Jack pulled to the curb directly outside Standiford's home. It would be impossible to travel any distance on foot with the inebriated Stark in tow, so this would have to do. Hopefully no insomniac would glance out his living room window as the two men were climbing out of the car and making their way to the rear of Standiford's home, but the risk couldn't be helped. At least it was Stark's own car and could not be traced to Jack.

Even in the worst-case scenario, if a neighbor spotted them and became suspicious enough to alert the police, Jack expected to be long gone by the time any squad cars showed up to investigate. He would only have a few minutes but that's all this should take.

He killed the engine and opened his door, having disabled the Monte Carlo's interior lighting before leaving the Cactus Motel. Stark's slack form slumped against his seatback, eyes half-closed as he softly hummed a tune Jack didn't recognize. His hands remained wrapped securely around the plastic cup, inside which a small amount of whiskey sloshed.

Jack crossed behind the parked vehicle and then opened the passenger door. "Time to go," he said softly.

Stark blinked and looked up, his eyes focusing on Jack with difficulty. "Go where?" he said, his speech slurred.

"You know the party we started back at your motel?"

Stark nodded.

"We're finishing it here." He hauled Stark out of the car by the arm, shoving the man against the doorframe after he wobbled to his feet. "In case you've forgotten," he said softly, "my gun is right here." He lifted Standiford's Walther and made sure Stark got a good look in the murky half-light. "Don't make a sound and don't try anything stupid or I'll drop you where you stand. Are you with me on this, Joel?"

Stark weaved and bobbed and after a moment, nodded tiredly. "I'm with you," he said.

"Then let's go." Jack eased the Monte Carlo's door closed, leaving the vehicle unlocked. He would have to return to the car before disappearing, in order to retrieve his bloody towel and the rest of his supplies, which would then be distributed among trash receptacles across Las Vegas.

He gripped Stark's right arm tightly at the crook of the elbow and they began walking/stumbling along Standiford's property line, paralleling his driveway and moving along the side of the garage. At the corner, they turned left and followed the contours of the house until reaching the back door.

"Sit down and be quiet," Jack commanded, his voice barely audible.

Stark said nothing, but he folded himself up and sat on the concrete back steps, closing his eyes and cupping his chin in his hands as he propped his elbows on his knees. He looked ready to pass out and Jack hoped he hadn't overdone it with the whiskey. All he needed was a few more minutes of consciousness from the man, then it wouldn't make any difference.

Satisfied he could safely divert his attention for the few seconds it would require, Jack removed his lock picking tools from his jacket pocket and bent over the lock. It was a simple design, cheaply made, providing little protection from a determined home invader who knew what he was doing.

Jack Sheridan knew what he was doing.

In seconds the lock was picked. Jack bent and whispered to Stark, "Stand up, Joel, I've got a little surprise for you."

Stark jumped slightly, almost as if he had forgotten his surroundings and situation. "Surprise?" he said, his fuzzy eyes narrowing with suspicion.

"Don't worry, it's nothing to worry about. In fact, I think you're going to like it."

Scowling, Stark heaved himself upright, somehow managing not to tumble off the steps. "What?" he said.

Jack leaned over and from an ankle holster, pulled a small Smith and Wesson 686 snubnose .38 revolver. He held it up for Stark's inspection and the man shrugged. "So what?" he mumbled. "You've been holding a gun on me for hours now. What difference is one more gonna make?"

Stark's eyes widened almost comically in surprise, though, when Jack spun it in his hand and offered it, grip first, to him. He reached forward hesitantly, clearly certain he was being baited into some kind of trap. About a foot from the gun he stopped moving and his hand hovered unsteadily in the air.

"What are you waiting for?" Jack said. "Take it. We don't have all night."

At that, Stark reached out and plucked the gun delicately out of Jack's hand, moving with deliberate drunken concentration. He held it in front of his face, examining it almost like a child trying to get a read on a vegetable he'd never seen before.

Then, moving more quickly than Jack would have expected given the man's advanced state of inebriation, he pointed the gun more or less at Jack's midsection and pulled the trigger.

The dry *click* sounded like a cannon shot in the early-morning desert quiet. Stark's shoulders slumped and Jack shrugged. "I told you you'd *like* your surprise, I didn't say you'd love it. You didn't really think I'd give you a loaded weapon, did you?"

Frustration and anger was evident on Stark's face. It flushed even darker than it had from the alcohol and he said, "What the hell am I holding it for, then?"

"You'll see," Jack answered, and opened Blake Standiford's back door, shoving Stark roughly into the dark house. The drunken man tripped over the threshold and crashed to the floor.

He lay there for a moment, stunned, and then he panicked. Shoved himself to his feet and staggered sideways, smashing into a wall and falling again.

Jack closed the door firmly, making no attempt at stealth. He wanted the occupant to hear them. Then he stepped over the flailing Joel Stark and disappeared into Standiford's living room. The layout of the mobster's house was fresh in his mind from this morning's scouting trip and he knew exactly where to go.

He eased against a wall and waited. This wouldn't take long.

31

Blake heard something.

A thud/crash downstairs woke him from his alcohol-induced slumber with a start, mid-snore, the darkness of his bedroom all-encompassing. He shook his head and the early-hangover pounding in his skull made him wince. What had he been thinking, drinking himself damned near into a stupor?

What time was it?

And more importantly, what the hell was that noise?

He squinted through fuzzy eyes at his digital clock, one of the early models with numbers printed on tiny cards that flipped down every minute as the time changed like a constantly scrolling rolodex consisting only of numbers.

Four-thirty.

He had been asleep—or, more accurately, passed out, he reminded himself—for an hour and a half and he needed a hell of a lot more rest and recovery time than that. His head pounded relentlessly and he felt as though someone had entered his bedroom while he slept and stuffed his mouth full of cotton batting.

But he had heard something, and it must have been something pretty significant to wake him up when he was this drunk. He wanted nothing more than to close his eyes and drop his heavy head back onto his pillow, but Blake Standiford had been a member of the Mercadante crime family for a long time and he knew better than most how dangerous this time of day could be, when potential victims were sleeping and unaware, ripe for the taking.

So he squeezed his eyes closed in concentration and listed, and was almost ready to assume he had been dreaming when he heard it again.

Another thump, this less obvious than the first but still clear.

Someone was inside his house.

Someone was inside his fucking house.

Holy shit, his situation was even more perilous than he had thought. Big Tony was cleaning house prior to Shotgun Sammy's men arriving in Vegas. That had to be it. He had sent one of his guys to take Blake out while he slept. The assassin was downstairs right now, getting the lay of the land, making sure there were no potential witnesses and familiarizing himself with an escape route as he prepared to put two slugs into his sleeping victim's head.

Suddenly Blake wished he had had nothing more to drink tonight than soda water or, even better, several cups of good, strong, hot coffee. His head pounded and his vision swam and he felt suddenly like vomiting, but his thoughts were surprisingly clear.

There was still a way out of this if he kept his cool.

He knew Big Tony's man—he wondered somewhere in the back of his mind who it was, not that it mattered, really—was here, and much more importantly, *Big Tony's man didn't know that Blake knew he was here.*

That fact gave Blake a small advantage, drunk or not. It wasn't even a small advantage, it was a *tiny* advantage, but it might be enough. If Blake could take out Tony's assassin, he should still have time to ambush the drug courier on its way into Vegas later today before hitting the road for parts unknown.

After all, if Blake was supposed to be dead, no one would expect him to rip off the family. It would be the perfect cover.

But he had to move fast, hangover or no hangover, drunk or sober, because Blake's advantage of surprise would evaporate quickly. He had to get downstairs and hit the hitter before the guy got his shit together and came up to finish the job.

The self-righteous anger began building, burning through Blake's alcohol-addled brain. Who the fuck did Tony Mercadante think he was? Did he not know by now that Blake was smarter and quicker and more devious than the rest of Tony's crew combined?

Well, he would damn well find out soon enough.

Tony felt for his gun. It was right next to his pillow where it had fallen out of his hand as he slept. He wrapped his fingers around it and grabbed a flashlight he kept next to his bed.

Then he began creeping slowly and quietly down the hallway toward the stairs. He held his gun in his right hand and his flashlight in his left. For now, the flashlight was off, held next to the barrel of the Ruger SR9 pistol, ready to snap on when the time was right. His heart was pounding and his mouth was dry, still filled with the cotton his incipient hangover had deposited while he was sleeping.

He didn't encounter the assassin coming the opposite direction on the stairway, and for that he was thankful. His goal was to get the drop on the man while the stranger was still getting his bearings in the first floor darkness.

The lack of light didn't bother Blake. He knew this house like the back of his hand. He'd grown up here, inheriting the home when his mother died in a household accident several years ago, when Blake had engineered a fall for the elderly woman down these very stairs after deciding he could no longer put up with her constant hectoring, her self-righteous judgment of him for his choice of career field.

The stairs were solidly build and carpeted, which meant they were quiet, and now that he had a plan, Blake moved with a sense of purpose that came close to matching his nervousness and fear. It seemed to take forever, but eventually he reached the bottom of the stairs.

Then he hesitated. Where would the assassin likely be?

Blake guessed the hitter was clearing every room on the first floor. The guy was being careful. It was what Blake would have done.

And if that was the case, Blake decided the hitter would clear the living room and dining room first. Then he would move through the kitchen and, once satisfied, climb the stairs to the second floor. It made the most sense, given the layout of the house.

And since at least two minutes had passed since Blake heard the sounds down here, the odds were good that the hitter was even now padding softly through the kitchen.

Moving this way.

His decision made, Blake wasted no more time. He moved to the swinging door that separated the kitchen from the foyer hallway, hesitated just long enough to take a deep, steadying breath, and then burst through the door and flicked on his flashlight.

And found himself face to face with a large man. The man looked young and was dirty and disheveled, like he had been rolling around on the ground, with dried blood crusting one side of his pockmarked face.

And the man was holding a gun.

His eyes were wild and red-rimmed he looked every bit as surprised as Blake felt, and he wasn't anyone Blake knew or even recognized and in a corner of his mind, Blake thought, *Where the hell did Tony dig this guy up?* and then he squeezed the trigger of the Ruger as the man was taking a step backward and the gun roared and the man staggered sideways as the surprised look on his face turned to shock, and then Blake fired again and the man went down in a heap on the kitchen floor.

He thrashed and kicked his heels, struggling to breathe through a chest with two 9mm slugs imbedded inside it, and then he coughed up a wave of blood and lay still.

Blake realized he was holding his breath, and he released it in an explosion. His hands were shaking and he felt sick to his stomach and his already pounding head felt like it might explode. He had killed before, many times, most recently the departed but unlamented Kathy Saldana, but in every instance he had felt totally in control, unthreatened personally.

This was different. This was a violation. This was some nameless scumbag breaking into his home to do him harm. He didn't recognize the guy, but Big Tony obviously possessed resources far beyond what Blake had given him credit for and was willing to plumb the depths of those resources to eliminate him.

He edged forward, shaking, cautious. The intruder was no longer moving, but Blake wasn't taking any chances. He stood over the motionless man, gun trained on him.

Bent down to pluck the hitter's gun out of his hand.

And froze as a second man rounded the corner from his living room and stepped into the kitchen.

The man had a gun.
And he was pointing it at Blake.

32

The look in Blake Standiford's eyes was one of utter, alcohol-and-adrenaline-fogged confusion. He was bent over, unmoving, hand extended toward Joel Stark as Jack rounded the corner. It was obvious the last thing he expected to see was a second intruder.

Jack closed the distance between them quickly, leveling his weapon at Standiford. The confusion in Standiford's eyes lasted a split-second, and then was replaced by a kind of calculated cunning.

And then the mobster started talking, speaking rapid-fire, saying anything he could think of to try to delay the inevitable. ""Don't shoot. We can make a deal. Whatever Big Tony's paying you, I can pay you more. I've got a big score planned for later today and I'll split the take with you, it's gonna be millions, it's gonna be enough to keep both of us rolling in dough for the rest of our lives, it's gonna be ..."

As he babbled, still bent awkwardly over Stark's unmoving body, the mobster eased the barrel of his pistol steadily upward. He was moving slowly, raising his left hand in surrender, presumably to divert Jack's attention from his other hand, which still held a lethal weapon. The angle of the gun was still wrong to present any danger to Jack.

Yet.

But that would change soon.

" . . . the delivery is just outside the city, and it's in just a few hours, and all we have to do is ambush the Mercadante guys with the money, take them out and then get out of town and we'll both be rich and we can split up then and we'll never have to see each other—"

Jack squeezed the trigger and a jagged crater opened up in Standiford's skull. A surprisingly delicate spray of liquid crimson flew right as the body tumbled left.

Jack fired again.

Standiford's body jerked as it dropped to the floor next to Stark and then lay still, surrounded by blood and tissue and bits of pulverized grey matter.

Jack moved quickly. His weapon had been fitted with a sound suppressor, but Standiford's had not, and while he doubted the neighbors were close enough to have heard the sound of the gun-fire—doubted they were even awake yet—there was no point in taking unnecessary chances, either.

He stepped outside the ring of devastation and leaned over, pressing two fingers lightly to Standiford's wrist, feeling for a pulse.

Nothing.

He waited a moment to be sure, then repeated the exercise.

Nothing.

Checked Stark in the same way.

Twice.

Nothing.

Both men were dead.

Jack lifted the unloaded Smith and Wesson off the floor next to the fallen Joel Stark and slipped it into his ankle holster. He wiped the Walther clean on his shirt and then pressed Stark's right hand around the grip, taking the time to manipulate the dead man's pointer finger to leave prints both on the trigger guard and the trigger itself.

Jack had fired the gun twice earlier in the day in anticipation of the two slugs he expected to put into Blake Standiford here tonight. A serious investigation would reveal pretty quickly that Stark had not been the one to shoot Blake Standiford, but Jack doubted any such serious investigation would take place.

From a law enforcement perspective, this crime scene would be nothing more than a deadly display of cosmic karma—two slime-balls getting what they deserved at each other's hands. The New

York rapist breaks into the home of the Las Vegas mobster for reasons unknown. Maybe a drug deal, maybe a robbery; nobody knows and they don't much care. Violence ensues and both men end up dead on the floor.

The fact that one of the dead men was the son of a New York cop might complicate matters for a while, but the investigation would quickly reveal Stark's despicable criminal history, and that history would likely outweigh the family law enforcement connection in the eyes of the local cops.

And even if it didn't, there was no way to tie the events to Jack, or—per the terms of the contract he had just fulfilled—to the Mercadante family. Investigators might have their suspicions; they almost certainly would, in fact. But in lieu of evidence to the contrary, the official line would have to be a robbery/home invasion gone bad. *And that's more or less true,* Jack thought, *except for the "gone bad" part.*

Jack released Stark's grip on the Walther and let it tumble to the floor. Then he dropped the man's unresponsive arm and it thumped down onto the tile next to the weapon. He thought about gathering up some cash or jewelry and filling Stark's pockets with it, then decided not to bother with what would be an unnecessary bit of overkill. So to speak. Time was ticking and he had already been here too long.

The authorities would either buy into the scene or they wouldn't, and in the long run it didn't matter anyway. Standiford was dead in a murder case that would be closed after a perfunctory investigation, and in the process Jack had managed to free Victoria Welling from a decade's worth of unrelenting of terror, giving her at least the chance for a happy—and safe—life.

He flipped on the kitchen light and looked over the scene one last time, and then shrugged. The gruesome sight should have horrified him, particularly given the fact he had orchestrated it.

But it didn't. He had no reaction to it at all, which he took as one more sign that maybe he it was time to begin considering a new line of work.

That was a concern for another day, though. Right now it was time—well past time, in fact—to leave. He retraced his steps to the back door and then eased through it, pulling it closed behind him. He hurried to Stark's Monte Carlo and retrieved his things, then disappeared into the night.

He had some walking to do.

33

Victoria stretched and yawned, blinking rapidly as the early-morning sun fought its way through the cheap shades of the Tumbling Dice Motel. For the first time in what seemed like forever, she actually felt refreshed in the morning, having benefitted from a full night's sleep, free from her usual nightmares and paralyzing fear.

She propped herself up on an elbow and glanced toward the door, expecting to see Harry Carson stretched out on the floor like he had promised he would be. Instead she saw a thin motel pillow and a couple of blankets in a pile, evidence Harry *had* been there, but he was currently nowhere to be seen.

She wrinkled her forehead in confusion. His strange post-two a.m. trip notwithstanding, he had struck her as dependable as a Swiss watch. If she hadn't felt that way she would never have considered allowing this virtual stranger to drive her to his motel, no matter how frightened she had been.

The old familiar fear began to build. The luxury of a good night's sleep, as refreshing as it was, didn't change the reality of her situation. Joel Stark was still out there, prowling Vegas and waiting for the opportune moment to do her harm.

Harry Carson had been a true gentleman, offering her the gift of one night's shelter from the unrelenting terror, a gift she had gratefully accepted. But Harry was here on business and he'd be leaving soon enough, maybe as soon as today. And when he left, Victoria would be no better off than she had been before meeting him. She would leave Las Vegas—probably today as well—and face a future of loneliness and fear, and of looking over her shoulder every minute of every day for the rest of her life.

The prospect was horrifying, and tears began to well up in Victoria's eyes. Dread lurked in her belly. She took a deep, cleansing breath, which helped almost not at all.

One day at a time. Get through today before worrying about tomorrow. It was a mantra she had been using for years, one that had prevented her from suffering a nervous breakdown at the thought of the maniacal rapist chasing her around the country. She prayed it would help her now, because she could feel the terror growing inside her like a metastasizing tumor.

Victoria tamped down the fear and slipped out of bed. She was so small inside the shorts Harry had given her to sleep in that she held the waistband with one hand to ensure they didn't simply slip over her hips and down her legs. She trudged to the window and pulled the curtain a couple of inches to the side, squinting against the glare.

Her heart skipped a beat as she spotted the now-familiar figure of Harry Carson crossing the lot, balancing a molded foam cup carrier in one hand, two lidded coffees jammed into it, and holding a paper bag in the other. She realized with a jolt of sudden surprise that she felt an uncomfortably strong attraction to this older stranger—a man she barely knew and who was clearly at least a decade her senior. It was a feeling she had not experienced in years and one she had given up on ever experiencing again.

Harry glanced toward the room as he approached and saw her peeking out the window. He gave her a wink and she felt a flash of embarrassment, like a child caught with her hand in the cookie jar. She let the curtain go and hurried to open the door.

"I'm not sure how you take your coffee," he said as he entered, "so this bag is filled with sugar packets and single-serving creamers. I took so many I thought the coffee shop was going to charge me extra."

Victoria accepted her cup with a grateful smile. She couldn't quite fathom Harry's ability to make her feel so at ease, but the fact was that he did. The sense of calm emanating from him was undeniable. They took seats across from each other at a small, round table and she pulled the lid off her cup, greedily inhaling the aroma of fresh-brewed coffee.

"I really needed this," she said. "I would have taken it any way you wanted to give it to me."

Harry grinned and she blushed. "You…you know what I mean," she added weakly.

"Why, yes, I think I do," he answered, refusing to let her off the hook. "But for now, at least, I think we should stick to breakfast and conversation, not that I don't appreciate the sentiment."

Victoria wished she could turn off the redness. Her face felt like one of the neon signs hanging in the windows at Tequila Mockingbird. She wondered whether her slip of the tongue was completely random or a manifestation of the attraction she was feeling.

"Anyway," Harry continued, "thanks for making my day. If you'll check inside the paper bag you might find a couple of cinnamon rolls. Not the healthiest of breakfasts, probably, but they'll give us something to munch on as we discuss your future."

Those simple words reminded Victoria of how silly she was being. Schoolgirl fantasies about the damsel in distress being rescued from by the mysterious stranger were appealing, but they weren't going to accomplish anything in terms of keeping her safe. Or even alive.

She shook her head. "I already know what my future holds," she said. "I'm going to leave Vegas as soon as I possibly can—hopefully by the end of the day—and head somewhere totally random. If I don't know where I'm going to end up, there's no way Stark can know, either. Once I get there—wherever 'there' is—I should have a few months of relative safety before he tracks me down again. When he does, I'll run. Again. If I survive."

Harry had started shaking his head when she was halfway through her statement. He had something to say, that much was clear, but rather than interrupting he waited patiently for her to finish.

Victoria raised her eyebrows. "What? Why are you shaking your head?"

He cleared his throat and sat back in his chair. Lifted his gaze and stared at a point in space over Victoria's shoulder. She was tempted to look behind her but knew there was only a dingy white wall back there. It was obvious Harry was trying to decide how to respond, and she sat silently, waiting, sipping her coffee.

"I understand how terrifying your life has been since your time in New York. But wouldn't you like to stop running? You said yourself how much you love Las Vegas and your job at Tequila Mockingbird."

"Of course I'd love to stop running. I'd like nothing better than to finally put roots down, and this is where I would choose to do it if I could. But that's just not feasible. If I don't move, and soon, I'll be dead or wish I was. You don't know Joel Stark. He's tenacious where I'm concerned. God only knows why. But he'll never give up."

"What if I told you Joel Stark can't hurt you any more? What if I gave you my word? You trust me, don't you?"

"Of course I trust you. I wouldn't have come back here with you last night if I didn't trust you, but I don't think you understand—"

Harry raised his hands. "Let me stop you right there," he said gently. "Hypothetically speaking, if I could *assure* you Joel Stark was no longer a threat to you, would you still want to leave Las Vegas?"

Victoria stared at this unusual stranger, the man she had come to trust so completely after such a short time, the man to whom she felt such a strong attraction. "Where did you go last night?" she asked quietly.

"I told you before, I had some business to attend to."

"In the middle of the night. While the rest of the world was fast asleep."

"Well, not the *entire* rest of the world. Vegas never sleeps. You live here, you must have learned that by now."

"You know what I mean."

Harry met her gaze steadily. "You never answered my question," he said, his tone as gentle as ever, his voice as soft as hers.

"Hypothetically speaking, huh?"

"Yes."

"Of course I'd stay in Vegas. I love it here, but—"

Again he interrupted her. This time his words were accompanied by a smile that took her breath away. "Would you do me one favor? Please?"

"What?"

"Don't leave yet. Stick around for another day or two before you go. If, after that time, you still feel you're in danger, by all means hit the road and don't look back. But in the meantime, keep a close eye on the news. I don't have a crystal ball or anything, but I get the feeling Mr. Stark's criminal tendencies may finally have caught up with him."

"Really? And why is that?"

Harry said nothing. He just waited, his eyes warm and his expression neutral.

Victoria thrummed the table with her fingers. "What did you say you do for work again?"

"I didn't. Not specifically. And I can't. But you said before that you trusted me. Has that changed?"

She thought about it.

Harry remained silent, letting her take as much time as she needed. He drank his coffee and watched her with his kind, expressive eyes, leaning back in his chair like he had not a care in the world.

"No," she said at last. "That hasn't changed."

"Good. You're a sweet girl and you deserve a long, happy life. I think it's about time you got started on it."

"But what—"

"How about these cinnamon rolls? Aren't they the best thing you ever tasted? I'd like to lift that bakery out of Nevada and take it home with me."

"Where's home?"

Harry just smiled at her, a tinge of sadness joining the deep well of kindness in his eyes.

34

Victoria Welling paced her tiny apartment endlessly. Harry had driven her to the otherwise empty parking lot at Tequila Mockingbird to pick up her car shortly after breakfast and their bizarre conversation, which was surely the strangest she had ever been a part of.

He then accompanied her back to the Royal Flush complex, assuring her that while she had no longer had any reason to be concerned about Stark, he understood her nervousness and would make sure she was safely locked into her home before leaving for the airport.

At her apartment doorway they had experienced the first—and only—awkwardness of their short relationship. Harry seemed uncomfortable, almost shy, utterly unlike the strong, confident man she had come to know.

"Remember," he said. "Give it a day or two before you bolt. Will you promise me that?"

"I promise," she said, already beginning to feel the tension humming through her body like a live wire.

"And turn on the TV and pay close attention to the news."

"I will."

Then he had wrapped her in his arms and hugged her tightly, kissing the top of her head although where she really wanted that kiss was on her lips. She had been alone and afraid for so long, though, that she had no idea how to communicate her desire to Harry Carson, so she simply enjoyed the sensation of warmth and safety for those precious few seconds, treasuring it like a miser treasures his cash.

His lips lingered for a few seconds and then he released his hold on her and turned toward the door.

"I'll never see you again, will I?" she asked his retreating form.

He turned, and when he did, the familiar smile—half-amused and half-sad—was etched onto his face. "You never know what tomorrow will bring."

He winked. And then he was gone.

*   *   *

She wasn't much of a TV watcher. Her tastes ran toward music and books rather than the surreal hyperactivity of television. But she did as he asked, leaving her small TV tuned to a local Las Vegas station, the volume low but not quite muted.

Time passed slowly, made doubly agonizing by the fact it was her day off at Tequila Mockingbird. Her plan had been to throw her meager belongings into the back of her little Pontiac and stop in at the club to quit while on the way to the interstate, leaving her old life behind—once again—by midafternoon.

Instead she paced.

She drank coffee and then, when she felt her nerves tightening and her body becoming jittery and even tenser than usual, switched to herbal tea.

And paced some more.

The noontime news broadcast provided no insight into why Harry Carson would have insisted she pay close attention to the local news, and as the afternoon dragged on, she began to doubt him. Why had she trusted him in the first place? The conviction in his voice had been plain, but he was gone now, and he wasn't coming back. The longer she stayed here, trapped like a bird in a cage, the easier it would be for Stark to hunt her down and do the things to her he had devoted his sociopathic life to.

She paced and drank tea and paced some more and, as the afternoon began to turn into evening, decided she needed a shower.

She felt hot and sweaty and nervous and wanted to wash off the fear that seemed to be seeping through every pore in her body.

The water was hot and the shower long and refreshing, and Victoria stepped into her threadbare Elton John towel just as the six o'clock news aired. She had turned the volume up on her television and the sound of the anchor's lead story floated through her closed bathroom door.

The bodies of two men were discovered this afternoon in a North Las Vegas home in what appears, at this hour, to be a home invasion gone wrong. Twenty-nine-year-old Las Vegas resident Blake Arthur Standiford III, rumored to be tied to the notorious Mercadante crime family, died inside his home sometime within the last twenty-four hours, apparently of gunshot wounds inflicted by a small-time New York drifter named Joel Stark.

Also killed in the altercation was Stark, as authorities theorize Standiford fired his own weapon at the intruder even as he lay dying on his kitchen floor. We go live now to correspondent Melissa Flowers, at the scene with breaking details.

A buzzing began to fill Victoria's ears and she felt dizzy and lightheaded. She slumped onto the closed toilet seat and the rest of the news report faded into meaningless background noise as she attempted to process what she had just heard.

Joel Stark was dead.

Exactly as Harry Carson had predicted.

Harry's words from less than eight hours ago came back to her, clear and precise. *I get the feeling Mr. Stark's criminal tendencies may finally have caught up with him.*

Dead.

Joel Stark was dead.

The lightheadedness began to pass and the buzzing in her ears faded, and she scarcely knew how to proceed. She would get dressed, of course. That was the first thing to do.

But then what?

Whatever she wanted.

The notion that she could now go anywhere she wished, and do anything she felt like doing once she got there—without fear of being harmed by the man who had haunted her nightmares for a full decade—would take time to sink in. A lot of time, probably. But already Victoria could feel her spirit lightening, with the weight of so much terror lifted for good.

She dressed slowly, puzzling through the mystery of Harry Carson and how he could possibly have known what took place at the home of some mobster she had never heard of in North Las Vegas, when he wasn't even from around here.

And what kind of businessman goes to work at two a.m.?

No legitimate kind, that was for sure.

But Harry Carson had a good heart; of that she was certain. He had listened patiently as she unburdened herself of her deepest fears. Had promised to protect her and had done so. Had even offered her his bed, not in a sexual way—although Victoria wasn't entirely certain she would have objected—but in a caring way. Had even predicted she would be free of the specter of Joel Stark, and had then been proven right.

There had to be a connection between the seemingly unrelated events of Harry Carson's appearance and Joel Stark's death. Coincidences of that magnitude simply did not happen.

But Harry Carson had a good heart. Of that she was certain.

He had told her she was going to have a future and now she did, however it had happened.

And it felt wonderful.

35

Mike Hogan sat in a bar inside one of the passenger terminals at Hartsfield International Airport in Atlanta, nursing a drink while waiting to board his connecting flight to Boston. The Harry Carson persona was long gone, along with his Harry Carson driver's license and credit cards, cut up and scattered across trash receptacles throughout the Las Vegas McCarran Airport.

The Organization spared no expense to provide numerous identities to its operatives when they traveled, the theory being it was much harder for the authorities to track three or four different people cross-country than it would be to track one.

Provided the operative proceeded with care.

And Jack Sheridan always proceeded with care.

So now he was Mike Hogan, and he sipped his drink and considered what he had done for Victoria Welling. Strictly speaking, eliminating one man while in town to fulfill a contract on another was against the rules, if professional assassins could be said to have "rules" in the first place. The Organization in general, and Mr. Stanton in particular, would not be happy if they discovered what he had done.

Still, Jack felt no regret. Victoria Welling's terror had been very real and very obvious, and Jack had no doubt every bit of the horror story she had related regarding Joel Stark was true. And if Stark had tracked her all the way across the country from Brooklyn, he most certainly was not in town to wish her well.

Besides, Jack *had* been given plenty of latitude in carrying out the contract. The details had been left to him, and Tony Mercadante's wishes—that Blake Standiford's elimination appear unrelated to his employment by the Mercadante family—had been served perfectly by the tableau Jack orchestrated in North Las Vegas.

Jack knew there was a very real possibility he had left a blood sample on Stark's clothing or inside his car. Certainly he had dripped blood on the carpet in Stark's motel room. But even if true, the samples would lead nowhere. The only way recovered DNA could come back to haunt Jack would be if he was taken into custody in the future.

The only wildcard in the entire operation was Victoria Welling herself. Jack had only known her for a couple of days. There was no telling how she would react once she learned of the death of her tormentor. She would be relieved, certainly, but she would also have a lot of questions, all revolving around the mysterious "Harry Carson," and the extreme actions he may or may not have taken to protect her.

It was possible she would take her suspicions, or at least her misgivings, to the local police. Jack didn't think that outcome was likely, but he could not deny it was at least a possibility.

Even if she did so, though, there was nothing to tie Jack to the events inside Blake Standiford's home. The guns used to kill the two dead men both belonged to Standiford, and Jack had been careful to wear gloves during both trips inside the mobster's home. Jack was known to Victoria only as Harry Carson, and even in the unlikely event the young pianist *did* go to the police and they *did* take her concerns seriously and they *did* investigate her mysterious protector, their trail would begin and end at the Tumbling Dice Motel on the south side of Vegas.

They would have Jack's description, of course, but so what? One of the reasons he had been so successful in his career was that he was entirely unremarkable-looking. Not ugly, not by a long shot. But he wasn't especially handsome, either. He stood average height, was thin but not skinny, muscular but not muscle-bound. He looked exactly like any one of a million American men in their mid-thirties.

And realistically, he doubted Victoria would ever visit the police. Every fiber of his being told him Victoria Welling would puzzle over the question of what Harry Carson might or might not have done, would spend many nights pondering the mystery, but would never take those questions any further.

She had been that fearful of Joel Stark.

Jack Sheridan's current alter ego Mike Hogan finished his drink and stood. He moved slowly and, he had to admit to himself, a little painfully. There was a reason careers in his chosen field were usually short, aside from the obvious possibilities of death and capture. The job was hazardous and physically demanding, better suited to a man in his early twenties than one in his mid-thirties.

After more than sixteen years spent operating as a military specialist and then as a civilian contractor, Jack was a dinosaur, and right now he felt as though he might just be teetering on the brink of extinction. His back ached, his muscles were sending an uninterrupted stream of complaints through his nervous system to his brain, and the gash on his face throbbed incessantly, covered as it was by only a gauze pad taped awkwardly to his face. Jack had to admit—if only to himself for now—that he was tiring of the professional assassin's life.

He moved through the terminal to his departure gate, painfully aware of the reactions of strangers, who, without exception, moved aside and averted their eyes as he approached. He wished he could convince himself it was only because of the facial injury, but he knew better. Killing people, even if those people were among the most vicious, dangerous and bloodthirsty on the planet, took a toll on a man's—or a woman's—humanity.

And once lost, that humanity could never be recovered.

He thought about Edie Tolliver, working her cute little butt off to make a success of the Three Squares Diner and provide for her adorable seven-year-old. He thought about her obvious attraction to him. He thought about how lonely he had become thanks to his desire not to expose anyone he cared for to the obvious dangers of his chosen career field.

He thought about all of that and moved a little more quickly. It was time to go home.

36

A steady drizzle fell from slate gray skies as Jack's flight from Atlanta touched down on Runway 4 Right at Boston's Logan International Airport. May could be a capricious month in New England, with the occasional scorching temperatures straight out of an August afternoon balanced off at times by freezing rain more appropriate to Thanksgiving than late spring.

Today's weather was closer to the latter than the former, and although only a few hours removed from the Nevada desert, Jack felt his time out west already fading into unreality.

The continuous throbbing in his cheek was sufficient reminder of Joel Stark's reality, though, as well as of Blake Standiford's and Victoria Welling's. Jack knew he would be foolish to consider any future contact with the pretty young piano player. He also knew that at some point, years from now, he would ignore common sense and take a quick trip out to Vegas, just to see how she was doing. From afar.

For now, though, he was satisfied. He had done all he could for Victoria. If nothing else, he had offered her a second chance at life, an opportunity she had clearly never expected, although richly deserved.

He wandered through the terminal building, carry-on bag slung over one shoulder, just another weary business traveler making his way home. Though he looked no different than the people surrounding him, he felt no kinship with them.

More than anything else, he felt alone. Utterly and completely alone. It was a sensation that invariably dropped over him like a wet blanket upon completion of a mission and one that was becoming more noticeable—and harder to ignore—as he grew steadily older.

The throng of travelers began to thin as he worked his way toward Central Parking. The air outside the terminal building was cool and brisk, the skies overcast, matching Jack's mood as the drizzle continued to fall.

He trudged to his truck and tossed his bag onto the empty passenger seat.

Then he sat for a long time, thinking, staring at nothing, before finally firing up the truck and heading for New Hampshire.

37

The Three Squares Diner was a whirlwind of activity as Jack walked through the door. The place always seemed to be busy on weekend mornings and today was no exception. He waited dutifully to be seated—as instructed by a sign just inside the front door—newspaper clutched in one hand, scanning the restaurant for one face in particular.

He didn't see that face right away. Nearly every table was occupied and the pair of waitresses on duty scurried around at double speed, working even harder than usual, which was saying something. Edie didn't have a lot of employees, but the ones she had were fiercely loyal to her and, like their boss, recognized the value of hard work.

After a moment Jack spotted Edie, her back turned, in the kitchen helping the overworked Three Squares cook deal with the morning rush. She was buttering toast like there was no tomorrow, and Jack grinned as he approached the cash register.

He raised his voice to be heard over the din of the busy restaurant and said, "What does a guy have to do to get a little service around here?"

Edie Tolliver spun on her heel, eyes flashing as she glared out toward the source of the complaint. "Just one moment, sir, and I'll—"

A broad smile replaced her look of impatient annoyance. She turned back to the beleaguered cook and said something Jack couldn't hear. The man nodded without looking up and Edie abandoned her post—just for a moment, Jack knew; he had seen this act played out before—and hurried through the swinging door to the register.

"Well, well, well," she said, wiping her hands on an apron that had somehow managed to remain snowy white despite her hard work in the kitchen. "If it isn't our very own world traveler. Decided to return to the scene of the crime?"

"I just couldn't stay away, the coffee's too good," Jack answered as Edie stretched up on her toes and kissed his cheek. "Fringe benefits aren't so bad, either," he said, mildly embarrassed by the attention but loving it.

The diners at the nearest tables, who had heard their exchange, chuckled and returned to their meals as Edie grabbed Jack by the elbow and turned him to face her straight on. She gasped and took a step back, concern clouding her beautiful blue eyes. "What the heck happened to you?" she said, tracing the gash lightly with her finger.

Jack had finally gotten the injury sutured last night after returning home, and the eighteen stitches it had taken to close the wound were joined by a nasty array of multi-colored bruises to make the right side of his face look like he had jammed it into a food processor.

"What, this little scratch?" he said lightly, removing her hand from his face and holding it in his. "Cut myself shaving, that's all."

"What do you shave with, a weed whacker? That looks deep."

They shared a laugh and Jack said, "It's not as bad as it looks, I promise. I can almost guarantee I'll survive. As long as I can get one of your world-famous omelets in me ASAP, that is."

Edie had begun squeezing his hand harder as their fingers were intertwined and it occurred to Jack out of nowhere that kissing this tiny, fiery, beautiful woman might be about the most important thing in the world right now.

So he did. He leaned her back on her heels, supporting her small body with his arms, and kissed her. It was hard and passionate, and after a half-second of undisguised shock—this was clearly not what Edie Tolliver had been expecting when preparing for work this morning—she returned his kiss with a fervor at least equal to his own.

They remained locked in an embrace for what felt to Jack simultaneously like hours and the barest fraction of a second. He became dimly aware of all sound fading away in the busy restaurant as patrons and workers alike stopped what they were doing and gazed in stunned surprise at the display unfolding at the front of the restaurant.

Approving whistles and a smattering of applause swept the dining room, and from a nearby table an elderly man with a head of hair nearly as pure white as Edie's apron piped up and said, "Does that come with the breakfast service? Because I was only having coffee, but if it does I'll take an order." He ducked as his wife swiped at him good-naturedly with one hand.

They finally pulled apart. "I suppose this might be a good time to ask if you'd be interested in dinner and a movie this weekend."

"I can't," Edie answered instantly, her face a blank. "I'm seeing someone."

Jack's heart fell into his stomach and then Edie burst out laughing. "Of course I'll go out with you! I've been waiting for this for years; I was beginning to think I'd have to kidnap you to get your attention."

He shook his head and grinned. For such a tiny woman, Edie Tolliver had an oversized personality and he loved it. "Well, you have my attention now. I'm pretty sure I won't be thinking about anything else for the rest of the week."

Edie laughed and Jack said, "Maybe we can find out what's playing that a seven-year-old would enjoy and bring Janie along." Jack had met Edie's daughter several times at the diner and the little girl was the spitting image of her mother, right down to the big personality.

Edie's eyes moistened, just a little. If Jack hadn't been standing so close to her he would never have noticed. "That sounds wonderful," she said.

He nodded happily. "It's a date then," he said. "In the meantime, I'll repeat my original question. What the hell does a guy have to do to get some service in this joint?"

He turned away, laughing, as Edie took a swing at his shoulder. She missed and nearly corkscrewed herself into the floor. "Now, now," he said. "None of that until at least the second date."

She grabbed his hand and led him through the crowded restaurant to an open table. He was still just as hungry as he had been when he walked through the front door, but Jack realized he felt better at this very moment than he had in a very, very long time.

Epilogue

The man sat alone at a table in the rear of the dining room, sipping coffee and picking at his breakfast. He had been sipping coffee and picking at his breakfast for over an hour, had accepted refills on his coffee twice and had been ready to call it a day and try again tomorrow when the target came strolling through the door.

Finally.

The man had been hanging around town for days, waiting for his target to show. He'd never been to this town, knew nobody in the diner. But he guessed his presence here wouldn't raise any eyebrows. A restaurant with food as good as this, located just a stone's throw off Interstate 93, likely saw a steady stream of strangers and near-strangers all the time.

And he had figured right. After three straight days of breakfasts, and after more than an hour spent loitering at his table today, not a single person had looked at him crosswise, fortunately for them.

He sat with his black trench coat folded neatly over his lap, his fedora placed on the table next to the wall, and watched his target as the man got chummy—extremely chummy—with the owner of the Three Squares Diner. It was a heartwarming sight, one that brought tears to his eyes and a half-smile to his hawk-nosed face.

The man with the black trench coat was a sucker for a happy ending, although he would never have admitted it to anyone except his ex, and nobody who knew him even peripherally was likely to believe it, anyway.

But the facts were the facts, and he had a tendency to cry at the end of even the most pedestrian love stories. It got to the point where his wife, back when she still *was* his wife, nicknamed him "The Faucet," a moniker that had annoyed the shit out of him but one that he had to admit, even now, had been justified.

So the man with the trench coat enjoyed this little impromptu love-fest as much as everyone else in the diner, even joining in the spontaneous applause that erupted during the enthusiastic lip-lock the couple shared way up by the front door.

This was interesting.

Very interesting.

And not just because the man firmly believed in the importance of love. It was interesting because all indications were that these two were either already a couple or were about to become one.

And that was a development of which the man had been previously unaware, despite what he believed had been exhaustive research into Jack Sheridan's personal and professional history, research that had included classified government documents supposedly destroyed years ago.

The man smiled and sipped his coffee as the obviously smitten owner of the Three Squares Diner took Sheridan by the hand and led him to an unoccupied table. He made a mental note to delve back into his Internet research the moment he left here. It was suddenly critical he find out all he could about this beautiful young woman.

All in all, he thought to himself, this apparent budding romance had to be considered a positive development. It was better than nearly anything he could have hoped for, in fact. If true, it would certainly make his job easier.

Because a lifetime of professional experience had taught the man that a person with nothing to lose is virtually impossible to control. And that made sense. Someone unconcerned with his own fate would have no incentive to respond to threats.

But a man in love, well, that was a different story entirely. A man in love would do just about anything to save the people he cared about, even if—maybe even *especially* if—he didn't care what happened to himself.

Very interesting, indeed.

The man with the trench coat drained his coffee and reached for his fedora, never taking his eyes off the happy couple trading barbs and smiling at each other no more than ten feet away. Sheridan had wrapped his arm protectively around the young woman's waist as they walked and she was looking up at him with shining eyes.

He dropped a twenty on the table and turned toward the door, squeezing past Sheridan and the unknown woman with a polite nod. He had work to do—specific work relating to this small business owner and her relationship to his target—and there was no time like the present, as his old man used to say. Before long he would know all there was to know about this suddenly important young woman, and then the plan he and his employer had hatched would begin coming together.

The man walked out the diner's front door into the bright May sunshine, trench coat folded over one arm. He thought about the impromptu reunion between Sheridan and the young woman and found himself tearing up again. It wasn't often you got to witness a truly spontaneous, loving moment like that. It had been a happy ending straight out of a Hollywood movie.

And he really did love happy endings.

Jack Sheridan returns in his second novel, *Trigger Warning: A Jack Sheridan Pulp Thriller*. To be the first to learn about new releases, and for the opportunity to win free ebooks, signed copies of print books, and other swag, take a moment to sign up for Allan Leverone's email newsletter at AllanLeverone.com.

Reader reviews are hugely important to authors looking to set their work apart from the competition. If you have a moment to spare, please consider taking a moment to leave a brief, honest review of *The Organization* at Amazon's *The Organization: A Jack Sheridan Pulp Thriller* page, at Goodreads, or at your favorite review site, and thank you.

Acknowledgements

I cannot state strongly enough how grateful I am for the love and support of my family. My wife Sue and my three grown children—Stefanie, Kristin and Craig—have been behind me fully and unquestioningly in my journey as a writer, and their support makes the toughest days bearable and the best days magical. My granddaughter Arianna isn't quite sure what to make of me writing books, but she loves reading them, and that's good enough for me.

Editor Dan Persinger is a no-nonsense guy. He's also knowledgeable, prompt and professional, and a man of the highest integrity. If you find an error in spelling, grammar or usage in this book, I guarantee it's either because I missed one of his edits, or I ignored it like the damned fool I am.

The cover art for *The Organization* was designed and rendered by Kealan Patrick Burke of Elderlemon Design. Kealan's a talented and award-winning author in his own right who also has been doubly blessed with incredible design skills. I told him I wanted a throwback cover, something that could have graced a pulp paperback genre novel from half a century ago. He delivered everything I asked for and more.

Last but never least, I want to thank you, the reader. Trying to carve out an audience in the minefield that is modern fiction writing can be a soul-crushing experience, but readers like you who shell out their hard-earned cash to give my work a chance are always in the forefront of my mind when I'm writing. You owe no writer anything, and I'm always humbled and appreciative when you consider my work worthy of your time.

Thank you for your continued support, and I'll talk to you again soon.

Also from Allan Leverone

Thrillers

Trigger Warning: A Jack Sheridan Pulp Thriller
The Lonely Mile
Final Vector
Parallax View: A Tracie Tanner Thriller
All Enemies: A Tracie Tanner Thriller
The Omega Connection: A Tracie Tanner Thriller
The Hitler Deception: A Tracie Tanner Thriller
The Kremlyov Infection: A Tracie Tanner Thriller

Horrow/Dark Thrillers

Mr. Midnight
After Midnight
Paskagankee
Revenant: A Paskagankee Novel Book Two
Wellspring: A Paskagankee Novel Book Three
Grimoire: A Paskagankee Novel Book Four
Covenant
Linger: Mark of the Beast (Written with Edward Fallon)

Horrow

The Becoming
Flight 12: A Kristin Cunningham Thriller

Story Collections

Postcards from the Apocalypse
Uncle Brick and the Four Novelettes
Letters from the Asylum: Three Complete Novellas
The Tracie Tanner Collection: Three Complete Thriller Novels

www.ingramcontent.com/pod-product-compliance
Lightning Source LLC
Chambersburg PA
CBHW071133200626
46817CB00018B/2936